Maggie licke[d]
turned away

It was bad enou[gh] [she was un]dressed. And the [sight of her tongue] wetting expectant lips was way too much to handle. How long would it take for lust to burn itself out anyway? Days? Weeks? *Months?* Hugo slumped into a chair at the end of the table with a sigh he had no hope of suppressing.

'You sound tired.' Maggie placed a bowl of porridge in front of Hugo and sat down to one side of him.

'I'm fine,' Hugo growled. There were six chairs at this table. Why did Maggie have to sit within touching distance?

'Have some cream.' Maggie's finger collected a blob of whipped cream as she passed him the bowl. She popped her finger in her mouth and sucked it clean with obvious relish.

Hugo closed his eyes in a very deliberate blink. Distraction was needed here. And it was urgent.

Alison Roberts lives in Christchurch, New Zealand. She began her working career as a primary school teacher, but now juggles available working hours between writing and active duty as an ambulance officer. Throwing in a large dose of parenting, housework, gardening and pet-minding keeps life busy, and teenage daughter Becky is responsible for an increasing number of days spent on equestrian pursuits. Finding time for everything can be a challenge, but the rewards make the effort more than worthwhile.

Recent titles by the same author:

CONSULTANT IN CRISIS
  (*City Search and Rescue* Book 1)
THE NURSE'S RESCUE
  (*City Search and Rescue* Book 2)
DOCTOR AT RISK
  (*City Search and Rescue* Book 3)
THE SURGEON'S CHILD
SURGEON ON CALL

A COURAGEOUS DOCTOR

BY
ALISON ROBERTS

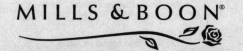

MILLS & BOON®

All the characters in this book have no existence outside the imagination of the author, and have no relation whatsoever to anyone bearing the same name or names. They are not even distantly inspired by any individual known or unknown to the author, and all the incidents are pure invention.

First published in Great Britain 2004
Harlequin Mills & Boon Limited,
Eton House, 18-24 Paradise Road, Richmond, Surrey TW9 1SR

© Alison Roberts 2004

ISBN 0 263 83902 8

Set in Times Roman 10½ on 12 pt.
03-0604-50719

Printed and bound in Spain
by Litografia Rosés, S.A., Barcelona

CHAPTER ONE

'YOU'RE needed, Hugh. A and E.'

'On my way.' Dr Hugo Patterson straightened, looping his stethoscope around his neck and smiling at the elderly woman in the bed. 'You've certainly picked up a bug, I'm afraid, Nancy. You're rattling away like an old train.' He patted the frail hand lying on the pale green coverlet. 'We're going to keep you on oxygen and start some antibiotics.' He looked up at the nurse standing nearby. 'Is the call urgent, Megan, or do I have time to pop in an IV line?'

'Sounded urgent.' Megan bit her lip. 'There was some shouting going on in the background and Lizzie sounded stressed.'

The look they exchanged acknowledged the unlikelihood of anything minor making Lakeview Hospital's nurse manager sound stressed. Hugo nodded as he reached for the chart to scribble instructions for the antibiotics he hoped would deal with his ninety-six-year-old patient's pneumonia.

'I'll be back to see you just as soon as I can, Nancy. You behave yourself in the meantime.'

'Thanks…love.' The effort of speaking at all was obvious but the smile she gave Hugo was as lovely as always. 'Go…they need you.'

'Are you happy to get the line in and start the medication, Megan?'

'I'll have a go.' Megan had to lengthen her stride to

keep up with the doctor. 'Her veins are horribly fragile, though.'

'I'll get back as quickly as I can. Have you heard how Nicola is getting on?'

'Last I heard she was six centimetres dilated and getting tired. I think Joan's a bit concerned about her.'

Hugo was moving faster now. 'I'll drop into Maternity on my way back here.'

It wasn't far to the somewhat ambitiously named A and E department of the small rural hospital. Hugo strode along the corridor without more than a passing glance through the long windows opening onto a wide verandah. Some of Nancy's fellow long-stay geriatric patients were ensconced in comfortable armchairs, enjoying the last fleeting warmth of the late winter's afternoon sunshine. This winter would undoubtedly be Nancy's last but Hugo was determined to pull her through this new bout of pneumonia so that she could enjoy for just a little longer the spectacular snow-covered peaks of the mountainous region she loved so much.

The double doors at the end of the wide corridor flapped in response to Hugo's firm push. The trauma room he was now in was curiously empty. This was their assessment and resuscitation area for serious injuries or illness, so where was the urgent case he had been summoned for? Hugo kept moving, through to the four-bed treatment room which led to the small reception and waiting area. He could hear Lizzie now, speaking with all the sternness and authority she had gained over her many years' nursing experience.

'You'll have to shift it. You're parked in the ambulance bay and there's an ambulance due to arrive any minute.'

'I'm not shifting. This is supposed to be a hospital, isn't it? Where's a bloody doctor when you need one?'

'Right here.' Hugo slowed his pace as he entered the reception area. His gaze took in Lizzie's arms, folded over her ample bosom, a man in belligerent stance with beefy hands gripping his hips, the open-mouthed fascination with which Anne, the receptionist, was watching the scene and finally the small tour bus parked in front of the ambulance loading platform.

'I'm Dr Patterson,' he added calmly. 'What seems to be the problem?'

The telephone began ringing just as both Lizzie and the man spoke at precisely the same moment.

'They're sick—the whole bloody lot of them,' the man announced impatiently.

'It looks like mild food poisoning to me,' Lizzie said. 'There's eleven of them.'

Anne's voice cut into the pause as Hugo held up a hand to request one speaker at a time.

'I've got Mr Payne on the phone, Hugh. He sounds very upset.'

'Lizzie?' Hugo tilted his head as he moved towards the desk, inviting the senior nurse to follow. 'Just give me a second with Mr Payne and then you can fill me in.' He took the phone from Anne. 'Hugh Patterson.' He listened for a few seconds. 'Try and calm down, Tom. How long has she been missing? Has she been unwell in any way today?' He listened again for a moment. 'If you don't find her in the next few minutes, call the police in to help. We can send an ambulance out as well if you need it.'

Lizzie was shaking her head as Hugo hung up. 'The ambulance won't be available for at least ten minutes. It's on its way back from Coronet Peak with a ski trauma. Erin Willoughby's broken her arm, snowboarding.'

'Oh, no!' It wasn't the first time Hugo had had cause to

regret working in such a popular location for adventure
sports of all kinds. It was easy to attract staff, especially
young nurses who had leisure pursuits such as skiing, but
it led to a high staff turnover and complications such as
staff shortages due to injuries like this. 'We're short-
staffed as it is.'

'I know,' Lizzie agreed grimly. 'And we're heading into
the winter peak season.' She glanced over her shoulder,
frowning. 'Where's that bus driver gone?'

Hugo could see where. Young Japanese tourists were
climbing off the bus, some clutching their stomachs and
some holding suspiciously full-looking paper bags. They
were all heading for the pedestrian entranceway to the hospital.

Lizzie followed his gaze and sighed heavily. 'I've told
him that we can't admit them all. I've talked to Jenny,
who's the GP on call for their hotel, and she's happy to
keep an eye on them. They'll be fine if they go to bed and
keep their fluid intake up.'

'Have you checked them out?'

Lizzie gave Hugo a look that suggested he should know
better than to ask such a question. 'Only half of them are
vomiting so far and the ones that have are feeling better
already. None of them are showing any signs of dehydration.'

'They're all very young.' Hugo smiled automatically at
the first couple entering the reception area but received no
response. One after another the tourists filed in, followed
by the driver.

'There you go,' he told them with satisfaction. 'They
just need something to stop them throwing up and we'll
get out of your way.'

'Stopping the vomiting will only keep them sick longer,'

Lizzie responded coolly. 'Their bodies are just trying to eliminate the toxin.'

The girl who approached them was looking very pale. 'Where is toilet, please?'

'Through there.' Lizzie pointed to the door at one side of the desk and the girl turned in the direction indicated. The queue for the single cubicle was instantly a problem.

'Anne, could you hand out some vomit containers, please? You might need to show some people through to a ward if they need a toilet as well. We're not going to cope with just this one.' Hugo turned to the bus driver. 'Are you the only one who isn't unwell?'

'Yep. That's because I didn't eat the picnic. I don't go for weird things like seaweed. I went to the pub and got a pie instead.'

'They stopped at Alexandra,' Lizzie explained. 'To eat the fish sushi they collected in Dunedin this morning. Everyone else ate the sushi and started getting sick within two hours. Five couples and the tour guide.'

'It's the ''Western Wedding Experience'',' the driver added helpfully. 'They have the white wedding in the stone church in Christchurch with full video recording and then they get the four-day adventure honeymoon. Ice-skating in Alex, gold mining stuff in Arrowtown—'

Anne was waving at Hugo. 'Mr Payne's on the phone again. They've found Mrs Payne but she's refusing to go home and she hit him in the face. He can't stop his nose bleeding.'

'Sounds like her Alzheimer's is getting worse,' Lizzie commented.

'It's too much for Tom to manage, no matter how much he wants to,' Hugo sighed. 'We'll have to get her in for assessment and look at a rest-home placement.'

A young man near the door groaned loudly and dipped

his face towards the white plastic bucket he held. Hugo felt like groaning himself but the bus driver was cheerfully ignoring any interruptions.

'There's two days in Queenstown to do the four-wheel-drive Skippers Canyon run with bungy-jumping, white-water jet-boat ride, skiing and so on. We're due for a dinner cruise on the lake tonight and…'

Hugo sucked in a deep breath. 'We'll send the ambulance out to check on the Paynes as soon as it arrives. Put Erin in the trauma room and keep our other visitors in Reception or the treatment room if any of them look like falling over.' His smile was apologetic. 'I'll have to leave you to it for the moment. We've got a delivery imminent that may need assistance and I've to check that Nancy's antibiotics are under way. She's got another dose of pneumonia.'

'Oh, no.' Lizzie's expression confirmed Nancy's status as one of the small hospital's favourite residents. She nodded. 'Don't worry. We'll hold the fort here.'

'I've already called Steve in to do the X-ray for Erin,' Anne told Hugo.

'Good girl.' For a recent school-leaver, Anne was proving very capable. She dimpled at Hugo's praise.

'I can help Lizzie look after this lot till you get back,' she added. 'Do you want me to call any of the other GPs in?'

'We'll see how we get on in the next half-hour or so,' Hugo decided. 'If things get any more chaotic than this, I'll definitely need some help.' He turned back to the driver who was, remarkably, still continuing his monologue.

'Then it's off to Te Anau, and the Milford Sound and dolphin bit, before heading back to Christchurch and the plane back to Japan.'

'Shift your bus,' Hugo instructed curtly. 'You'll find a

parking area outside Outpatients to the right of the ambulance bay.'

The maternity suite beckoned like an oasis of calm in a day that had deteriorated at an alarming rate. The midwife, Joan Pringle, was outside the door of the delivery room when Hugo arrived. Her white uniform looked as crisp and fresh as it had first thing this morning and her long blonde hair was still neatly coiled at the back of her head, with no errant tendrils to spoil the young woman's aura of competence. Joan's even features were as pleasing as the rest of her appearance, and her pale blue eyes never failed to be a little surprising. At present, however, the midwife's smile was strictly professional.

'Good timing, Hugh. I think the pethidine is wearing off. The entonox doesn't seem to be providing enough additional relief any more.'

'How's it looking?'

'Seven centimetres last time I checked, maybe eight. And that was twenty minutes ago so we shouldn't be far off transition. She's getting very tired, though. I think she might need some help. I've got the ventouse and forceps kits ready but I won't call you until I know for sure.'

'I'm glad you're in charge here, Joan. It's going mad everywhere else at the moment. Roll on Friday.'

'I'm looking forward to it as well.' Joan's smile was less professional this time and it took Hugo a second to realise she was referring to their customary Friday night date and not the end of his week on full-time hospital cover that he had been referring to. He returned the smile, feeling a trifle guilty that the date hadn't been a priority.

Nicola Cross, doing her best to deliver her second child, was delighted to see Hugo.

'I'm so glad you're still on duty, Dr Patterson.'

'I would have come in for this anyway, Nicky. And I'm

never far away.' His smile was a little wry as he noted the healthy rate of beeping from the foetal heart-rate monitor. 'Sometimes I think I should have bought a house a bit further on around the lake.'

'You got part of the old Spencer farm, didn't you?' Nicola seemed eager to distract herself from the prospect of another contraction.

'Yes. I was lucky enough to get a stretch of lakeside with the old shearers' quarters and the woolshed.'

'Is it true that some hotel chain offered Mrs Spencer millions for it?' Nicola's husband, Ben, was sitting beside the bed.

'She certainly could have done a lot better than selling it to me, but she knew how much I loved the place.' Hugo smiled fondly. 'I inherited her dogs last year. Maybe she wanted them to live out their lives on a patch of their own land.'

'Hugh's converted the shearers' quarters,' Joan added. 'It's a beautiful little house now.' She turned away to wash her hands and Hugo couldn't help wondering if it had been the mention of the dogs that had prompted such laudable thoroughness in her technique. Despite some valiant efforts, Joan had never been able to hide her dislike of any domestic pet's less hygienic attributes.

Nicola wasn't listening any more. She had put the entonox mask to her face and was sucking in long breaths of the pain-relieving mix of oxygen and nitrous oxide.

Hugo waited until the contraction was over to examine Nicola. 'You're almost fully dilated,' he told her. 'So it shouldn't be too much longer. It means I can't give you any more pethidine, though, because it might affect the baby's breathing.'

'I'll cope,' Nicola said wearily. 'As long as I know it's

going to be over soon.' She groaned and pulled the mask to her face. 'Here we go *again.*'

'I thought it would be easier the second time around.' Ben had risen to put his arm around his wife's shoulders for support. Nicola wrenched the mask clear.

'It was no picnic the first time, mate.'

Her choice of words was enough to prompt Hugo to move on. He would have to race up to the ward to check Nancy and then get back to see how Lizzie and Anne were coping with the aftermath of the sushi picnic.

Nicola's mother was outside the delivery room. She appeared to be having difficulty retaining her hold on a two-year-old boy's hand.

'We've been around the car park three times,' the older woman sighed. 'There aren't any more aeroplanes taking off over the road and Henry's bored.'

'Wanna go in the *bus*,' Henry informed Hugo.

'No.' Hugo shook his head firmly. 'It's a nasty, smelly bus. You wouldn't want a ride in that.' He smiled at Henry's grandmother, ignoring her faintly astonished expression. 'It shouldn't be too much longer before Henry's brother or sister turns up. I'll be back soon.'

'Soon' was fortunately an elastic expression. Megan hadn't managed to get an IV line into Nancy so Hugo spent nearly fifteen minutes in the ward, coaxing an ancient vein to accept a cannula large enough to carry fluids and the hopefully life-preserving medication. Back in A and E, the break in Erin Willoughby's forearm had been X-rayed by Steve, the technician.

'Nice clean break,' Hugo pronounced. 'We can reduce and set that, no problem, so we won't have to ship you off to the big smoke.' He shook his head sadly. 'How could you do this to us, Erin? You know how short-staffed we are.'

'Sorry, Hugh.' Erin's wide smile removed some of the sincerity from her repentance. 'But you should have seen the air I was getting with my jumps before I canned out. It was awesome!'

Thanks to the entonox, Erin's smile was still apparent even when Hugo and Lizzie straightened her arm and applied the first layers of plaster bandages.

'I'll leave you to finish, Lizzie, and get another X-ray done. Sorry—it's going to make you a bit late getting off duty.'

'No problem,' the older nurse assured him. 'Can you just make sure Anne's coping in Reception before you disappear again?'

Anne was coping admirably. She had provided a cup of tea for the bus driver and they were having an animated conversation in front of the silent, pale audience that filled all the seating the reception area had to offer.

'So they come all the way to New Zealand just to do the white weddings?'

'They have another ceremony in Japan later. Or maybe they do it first.' The driver's shrug indicated the unimportance of the order. 'It's great business, anyway. I do the honeymoon run every couple of weeks now.'

Hugo ran an experienced eye over the exhausted and somewhat bewildered-looking audience. 'Things seem to have settled down here.'

'Nobody's been sick in the last twenty minutes.' Anne nodded. She lowered her voice. 'I think Jess might need danger money when she comes in to clean the loos tonight, though.'

'Can't say I'm looking forward to cleaning up my bus either.' The driver drained his mug. 'All part of the job, I guess, so I'd better get on with it. Thanks for your help, Doc.'

'You're welcome. I don't think anybody will be wanting to go bungy-jumping or jet-boating tomorrow. They all need a good rest and an intake of clear fluids. Tell the tour guide to call a doctor if she's worried about anyone later. The hotel management will be able to help.'

Walking down the corridor again, Hugo could see the young honeymooners shivering as they climbed back onto their bus. Night had fallen with winter's dramatic sudden-ness and, judging by the spectacular red glow silhouetting the top of the craggy mountain range, it was going to be an icy one. Winter Festival participants would be happy with the fine day that tomorrow would undoubtedly bring. Apart from Erin, of course, who would no longer be par-ticipating in any freestyle snowboarding competition.

No summons had come from Maternity and Hugo was not surprised to find that Joan had managed a potentially difficult birth without his assistance. He arrived at the de-livery suite again to find an extended and happy family crowding the room.

'It's a girl,' Ben informed him solemnly. 'I got to cut the cord.'

'Congratulations—she's gorgeous.' Hugo's admiring gaze gave no indication that he was assessing the new baby's condition. 'Have you chosen a name?'

'*Mannie*!' Henry shouted.

'Melanie,' Nicola corrected with a tired smile. 'Do you want to give your sister a kiss, Harry?'

'No.' Henry wriggled in his grandmother's arms. 'Man-nie's dirty.'

'She just hasn't had her bath yet.' Joan caught Hugo's eye. 'Apgar score at one minute was nine and it was ten at both five and ten minutes.'

Hugo smiled at Melanie's proud parents. 'Sounds like

she's fine,' he said. 'I'll check her properly when you've had some more time for a cuddle.'

'Nicky might need a couple of stitches but it's only a small tear.'

'Placenta intact?'

'Appears to be. It's over there if you want to check.' Joan nodded towards a covered basin on the trolley. Hugo reached for a pair of gloves as Henry began drumming his small heels against his grandmother's legs.

'Wanna get *down*.'

If Hugo had been a little quicker he might have rescued the basin before Henry tripped and fell against the trolley, which tipped over with a resounding crash. The small boy howled with fright, his new sister took up the cry and the rest of the family looked alarmed. Joan's smile was tight. She picked up the toddler and deposited him firmly onto the chair beside the bed.

'Sit on this chair, Henry. And don't move!' She leaned down. 'If you're a good boy and stop crying right *now*, I'll see if I can find you an ice block.'

Henry hiccuped as the sobs subsided. Hugo scooped up the mess on the floor, silently applauding Joan's ability to deal with small children. It was disturbing to find he was now looking forward to leaving work so eagerly but there was just so much a man could take in one day. Grandma took Henry home, Hugo stitched up Nicola's tear and Joan took the baby to the nursery to clean her up. Hugo joined her and pronounced the baby fit and healthy after a thorough paediatric check. He watched as Joan expertly applied a tiny disposable nappy and then swaddled the tiny girl in a soft cotton blanket.

'You make that look so easy.'

'It is easy.' Joan tucked the baby into the crook of her elbow and smiled at the infant. 'Isn't she gorgeous?'

'Absolutely.' Hugo couldn't quite put his finger on the reason for his sudden unease. Maybe it was because it was taking so long for him to escape.

'Do you know, I've delivered more than a hundred babies since I came here?'

'Really? I guess you would have. You've been here nearly three years and we get about ninety births per annum.' He smiled admiringly. 'You're doing your fair share, that's for sure. Are you still enjoying your job?'

'Oh, I love it.' Joan's smile was rather wistful, however.

'But?'

Joan hesitated. The glance she gave Hugo seemed almost shy. 'I guess sometimes I wonder how many more of these bundles of joy I'll deliver for other women before I get one of my own.'

Hugo's unease deepened perceptibly. 'You're only thirty, Joan. There's plenty of time…isn't there?'

'Of course.' Joan had hesitated just long enough to let Hugh know that, as someone who cared, it was his duty to investigate this matter further. His sigh of relief as his pager sounded was fortunately not audible.

'I'd better get that.' The atmosphere became safely professional again. 'I'll catch you later when I check on Nicola again. Maybe we'll have time for a coffee before you go home.'

'You'd better get your skates on, then.' Joan glanced up at the wall clock. 'I've got my oil-painting class at eight o'clock and I can't miss that again.'

Hugo didn't really need to spend twenty minutes in the long-stay geriatric ward, making sure that Nancy was as comfortable as possible and that the night nursing staff would continue her close monitoring. Neither did he need to do such a thorough check on the four general medical patients they had at present. The trip to A and E to send

Erin home with some pain relief and instructions on caring for her arm was not entirely necessary either, but each task he set himself seemed perfectly prudent. It certainly hadn't been his intention to take so long getting back to Maternity.

'Has Joan gone home, then?' he asked the night nurse.

'Twenty minutes ago. Did you want her for something?'

'No.' Hugo was disconcerted to find a hint of relief rather than disappointment lurking. He must be more tired than he'd thought. 'How's Nicola?'

'Sound asleep—just like her daughter. Do you want to see them?'

'I won't disturb them. It's high time I went home myself.'

The road curved around the edges of Lake Wakatipu and Hugo found himself nurturing his first real hope of winding down from a long and tiring day. The level of stress he was trying to escape was unusually high. He loved his job and his lifestyle and it was a rare occurrence to have a day as hectic as today's had been. The busload of poisoned honeymooners had tipped the balance a little too close to chaos for comfort but the diverse range of illnesses and injuries that tourists to the area brought was part of what kept his life as a rural doctor so interesting.

And the tourists were flocking to Central Otago, and Queenstown in particular, in increasing numbers every year. More than once the alpine resort had received accolades of being the friendliest foreign city and it was the only New Zealand destination to rank amongst the world's top twenty. A place of enormous scenic beauty, with a rich gold-mining history and award-winning vineyards, Queenstown had also earned a reputation as the adventure capital of the world. With a baseline population of fewer than twenty thousand people, peak summer and winter tourist seasons could take numbers to over forty thousand. That dramatically increased the workload of the available GPs and the local hospital where Hugo worked for most of his time as its on-call physician and medical administrator.

Two startled rabbits ran from the beam of the headlamps as Hugo turned to swing his Jeep into the covered space the old woolshed provided for his vehicle. Three old farm dogs competed for his attention the moment he stepped out, and Hugo bent to fondle three pairs of ears before making his way to the long, low house sitting only metres away from the lake-side shingle beach. Having reached the veranda, he paused for a moment despite the bone-chilling temperature to take in the shimmer of moonlight gilding the glassy, black surface of the lake. It was bright enough to make the lights of Queenstown on the far shore of little note.

The happy panting of the dogs and the gentle rub of shingle from tiny waves at the lake's edge were the only sounds to break a deep and peaceful silence. Then a muted whine from one of the dogs reminded Hugo that he was very late producing their dinner. He moved inside, checked his phone for messages, opened the logburner to add wood and crank up the air flow and then filled the three bowls in the laundry with dog nuts. Reaching into the fridge to retrieve the remains of last night's casserole for himself, Hugo spotted the half-finished bottle of white wine. One glass wouldn't hurt, even if he was on call. The only message on his phone was from his mother and Hugo had an uneasy feeling that talking to Gwen Patterson might not be the best way to try and unwind.

In fact, it might be better if he put off returning the call until tomorrow. Leaving the bottle where it was, Hugo put the casserole in the microwave and hit the reheat button. The old leather armchair near the fire looked extremely inviting and Hugo took his plate in that direction a few minutes later. The phone was within reach, recent, unread copies of his favourite medical journals were on the coffee-table beside the chair and his dogs were lying contentedly in the circle of warmth. Hugo felt his stress levels declining rapidly. He was, once again, a very happy man.

At least, he was until the insistent call of the telephone jerked him from a very pleasant post-prandial doze.

'Darling, you're finally home! I rang earlier.'

'I was just thinking about you,' Hugo said in surprise. The half-dream had been a less pleasant aspect of the doze. He had been almost convinced that his mother was about to arrive on his doorstep for another extended visit—intent on finding the woman who would bear her grandchildren. As much as Hugo loved his mother, anything more than a three-day visit was a daunting prospect. 'I've been incredibly busy today,' he added hurriedly. 'In fact, life is generally a bit hectic at the moment.'

'Don't worry, Hugo. I'm not planning a surprise visit. Queenstown's far too cold for me in winter.'

'It's freezing,' Hugo agreed. 'But the mountains are looking glorious with all the snow.' He relaxed a little. 'How are you, Mum?'

'Oh, I'm fine.' The fact that Gwen had something more important on her mind than the list of minor, age-related physical ailments she loved to discuss with her son, the doctor, was a warning. That she had rung twice in the space of two hours made the matter of some urgency.

'Is everything OK at home?'

'Oh, yes. Everything's fine. Apart from the fridge. It's making a very funny noise. Sort of a clunk and then a dribbling sound. It always seems to happen in the middle of the night.'

'Are you not sleeping well?' Talking about fridges reminded Hugo of that bottle of wine. He pushed himself slowly to his feet.

'I'm fine,' Gwen repeated impatiently. 'I didn't ring up to talk about me, dear.'

'Who did you ring up to talk about?'

'Maggie Johnston.'

Hugo sat down again abruptly. And silently.

'Are you still there, Hugo?'

'Of course. Did you say Maggie Johnston?'

'Don't tell me you've forgotten who she is?'

'No.' Hugo's tone was cautious. 'I haven't forgotten.'

The silence spoke volumes. A single instant that managed to cover so many years. A wealth of memories, both happy and sad. Flashes of grief. Of laughter. Of a lifetime left well behind now.

'I keep in touch with her mother, you know. Eleanor and I always exchange Christmas cards. She rang me up yesterday. Or was it Monday? Anyway, she wanted to talk about Maggie.'

'Why? Is she in some kind of trouble?'

'Oh, no! Nothing like that. She's coming to Queenstown. On Friday. I told Eleanor she could stay with you, dear.'

'*What?*' Hugo stood up again and this time he kept moving. Towards the fridge. 'What did you tell her something like that for?'

'They're old friends, Hugo. Almost family. You know how close we all were once.'

'That was a very long time ago,' Hugo reminded his mother. He shook his head. 'She's coming *this* Friday? What for? Does she ski?'

'I didn't ask Eleanor about skiing. Does it matter?'

'No.' Hugo gritted his teeth as he opened the fridge. 'I just wondered why she was coming.'

'Oh. She's got a new job.'

Hugo extracted the bottle of wine. 'What's she doing these days?' He reached for a glass from the cupboard as a horrible thought struck. 'Didn't I hear years ago that she had gone nursing?' They were trying to recruit nursing staff at his hospital. The prospect of having to *work* with Maggie Johnston was alarming to say the least.

'Yes, you're right.' Gwen sounded surprised. 'I'd forgotten that. But she's not nursing now…I don't think.'

Hugo pulled the half-inserted cork from the bottle with his teeth and poured what he hoped would be a reviving drink. There was no point trying to jog his mother's memory. She would be happy to agree with whatever he suggested and prepared to conclude that whatever it was was probably correct.

'Eleanor said something about driving. Yes, I'm sure that was it. Maybe she's driving a truck.'

'It wouldn't surprise me. Probably something articulated and weighing in at about twenty tons.'

'That's a bit heavy for a girl, isn't it?'

'Maggie's not a girl, Mum. She's a grown woman.' Hugo's mental calculation was swift. He was thirty-six. His sister Felicity and Maggie had both been six years younger. 'She's thirty years old, for heaven's sake,' he grumbled. 'She doesn't need someone looking after her. I'm sure she's perfectly capable of finding her own accommodation. She's probably quite happy to pitch a tent on the side of the road if she has to.' Hugo breathed a sigh of relief. 'In fact, those large trucks usually have a sleeping compartment behind the driver's cab. I'm sure I could find her a place to park it.'

'Oh, no! That wouldn't do at all, dear. I don't think she *owns* a truck. She just drives…something. Eleanor said she's been trying very hard to find a house to rent but they're as scarce as hen's teeth and ridiculously expensive.'

There was no hint of relief in Hugo's sigh this time. Queenstown was notorious for a lack of rental accommodation during peak tourist periods and for outrageous prices at most times. He could well remember his own delight in purchasing a property of his own. His own home. Where he lived, quite happily, by himself.

'There's always motels. I'm sure I could find an available room.'

'That's what Eleanor suggested.'

Good for Eleanor, Hugo thought. At least someone was on his side.

'But I said, ''Don't be ridiculous, Nelly. Why should she pay a hundred dollars a night when Hugo has a spare room and he's living there all by himself. Lonely.'''

'I'm not lonely, Mum. I keep telling you how happy I am.'

'You're still living by yourself, dear. It's not natural—not at your age. You should be settled down with a nice little family by now. Do you know I'm the only person in my bridge club who doesn't have *any* grandchildren?'

'You have mentioned it once or twice.'

'Some of them have *ten*!'

'I'm working on it, Mum.'

'I'm seventy, Hugo. And last time I checked I wasn't getting any younger.'

The reference to a biological clock struck a disturbing note that distracted Hugo momentarily. Where had he heard something like that recently? 'You don't look anything like seventy,' he said. Maybe some flattery would help him change the subject. 'Are you keeping up with your yoga classes?'

'Of course. Don't try and change the subject, Hugo.'

'As if I would.' Could, Hugo amended silently with a wry grin.

'How long is it that you and that girl have been seeing each other? You know who I mean. Jenny. No, Jane.'

'Joan,' Hugo supplied. He took a long swallow of his wine. That was it. It had been Joan's biological clock he'd heard ticking today. 'And we've been friends for about a year now.'

'Are you going to marry her?'

'Marriage isn't something to rush into, Mum.'

'I rushed into it with your father. We had sixteen very happy years together. Your dad had two beautiful children by the time he was your age.'

The short silence was weighted by the memory of his father's premature death when Hugo had been only fourteen. At least Gary Patterson hadn't had to live through the tragic loss of his teenage daughter. A daughter who would probably have obliged by producing at least a few grandchildren by now.

'I'll see what I can do,' Hugo said placatingly.

'You would have married her by now if she was the right woman,' Gwen suggested brightly. 'Maybe you should keep looking for a bit.'

'I don't have time to go out hunting for women.' Hugo was annoyed by his mother's inadvertently perceptive observation. Striking up a friendship with Joan had been almost inevitable due to her availability as a nurse in his hospital. The relationship had become a reasonably comfortable habit until very recently. Possibly today, in fact. Joan's comment about her age and babies had probably made him uneasy because it reminded him of his mother.

And now his mother was making him uneasy by sowing a seed of doubt about the liaison that suddenly seemed familiar enough to have been around, unrecognised, for some time.

'I don't think Maggie's married.'

Hugo's huff of laughter was incredulous. 'Mum! Maggie's a—' He stopped short. OK, he hadn't seen Maggie for more than ten years and she hadn't really stepped out of 'kid' category then, but she was a grown woman now. He'd said as much himself and far too assertively to go back on. And he didn't want to go back on that statement. Kids needed looking after. They needed a place to stay. 'Maggie's family,' he amended hurriedly. 'Or close enough, anyway. Like you said yourself.'

'Exactly!' Gwen sounded triumphant. 'That's why I knew you wouldn't object when I told Nelly Maggie could stay with you.'

Hugo's groan was silent. If he changed his tune and objected that Maggie wasn't really in their extended family, his mother would have her pegged as a potential mother for her grandchildren. Either way, he was in for some feminine emotional blackmail that he really didn't have the energy to contend with. He drained his glass of wine.

'Fine,' he growled reluctantly. 'She can stay.'

'For as long as she likes,' his mother finished helpfully.

'For as long as it takes her to find a suitable permanent arrangement,' Hugo corrected firmly.

'I knew you'd be happy about it.'

'I didn't say I was happy.'

'Nelly will be so pleased.' Gwen appeared to be ignoring his comments. 'I think she worries about Maggie more than she lets on.'

'Somehow—' Hugo was unaware of the wry expression on his features '—that really doesn't surprise me.'

CHAPTER TWO

BLACK ice.

The small car lost traction and went into a skid, turning a full three hundred and sixty degrees before careening sideways into the solid rock wall of the gorge. Maggie Johnston braked her own vehicle gently, negotiating the curve around the crashed car until she had gone far enough to be easily seen by oncoming traffic. She hit the hazard light button on her dashboard and then pulled the release catch for the hatch at the back of her car. Thank goodness she had unearthed her first-aid kit before stuffing in any more of her worldly possessions now filling all the available space.

And thank goodness the car had skidded towards the solid side of this tortuous road. Had it gone the other way it would have tumbled about fifty metres into the impressive flow of the Cromwell River that sliced through the base of this picturesque gorge. Maggie wasn't thinking about the setting's scenic qualities right now, however. Having alerted the emergency services of the incident, she was now assessing the hazards the scene presented. Her own car would warn traffic of the obstruction on that side of the road around the bend. The narrow section in the direction she was now walking was relatively straight and…yes, there was another vehicle approaching with due caution. Maggie waved her arms and the driver stopped and rolled down his window.

'Is anybody hurt?'

'I'm about to find out.' Maggie's air of control was unconscious. 'Could you park your car back at the next bend and put your hazard lights on? Wave down any approaching traffic and warn them to stop.'

'Have you called an ambulance?'

'It's on its way. I just need to find out exactly what we're dealing with.' Maggie was already moving away swiftly. 'Don't worry, I know what I'm doing. I'm a paramedic.'

It was only a minute or so after the accident that Maggie reached the passenger's door of the crashed car, which was accessible. The occupant on that side was sitting there, clearly stunned by what had happened. Maggie tried the doorhandle but the front of the car was crumpled enough for it to have jammed. She noted that no airbags had been deployed as she tapped on the window.

'Hello, can you hear me?'

The woman's head turned and she blinked at Maggie in bewilderment.

'Can you roll your window down?' Maggie called. 'I can't open the door.'

The woman moved quickly now and the window lowered. Maggie leaned in so that she could see the driver as well.

'Hello, there. Are either of you injured?'

'I…I'm not sure,' the driver stammered. 'I don't know what happened.'

'You hit a patch of ice,' Maggie told him. 'Your car skidded and hit the wall.'

'Oh, God!' The middle-aged woman burst into tears. 'We could have been killed.'

'It's OK,' Maggie said. 'You're safe. My name's Maggie and I'm a paramedic. Can you tell me if you have any pain anywhere?'

'No.' The woman was struggling to release her safety belt. 'I want to get out.'

'My neck hurts,' the man said. 'And I'm bleeding. I've cut my arm.'

'Try and stay still,' Maggie instructed. She couldn't see any evidence of major ongoing blood loss and neither occupant was showing any signs of breathing difficulties. She looked at the car again. It was a three-door hatchback very similar to her own so it was going to be difficult for anyone to climb into the back and provide support for a potential cervical injury. The passenger door was jammed and the driver's door was blocked by the rock wall it rested against. She looked past the car to the group of people approaching.

'Does anybody have a crowbar or something similar?' she called. 'I need to try and get this door open.'

'Let me try.' A large man stepped forward. He reached for the door catch and pulled. Maggie saw him frown as he reassessed the situation. She picked up her mobile phone and made contact with the emergency services again.

'We have two people trapped,' she informed them. 'One appears to be status 4, the other status 3 with a possible cervical injury. We need the fire service, a tow truck and an ambulance.' She glanced at the growing number of onlookers. 'We're probably getting a bit of a traffic jam on the road as well.'

The man trying the door was now gripping the windowframe as the passenger held the catch open from the inside. He had his foot against the bottom of the car and with each pull the metal was giving a little. As Maggie finished her call the door was finally wrenched open enough to allow the woman to escape. She was still sobbing and Maggie gave her over to the care of the bystanders with instructions to keep her warm as she opened her first-aid kit and then climbed into the vehicle.

'Is your car fitted with airbags?'

'Just on my side. Why hasn't it gone off?'

'I don't know.' Maggie reminded herself to be careful until the fire service arrived with a cover for the steering-wheel. Getting between an injured occupant and a deploying airbag had killed more than one paramedic since their introduction.

'Are you having any difficulty breathing at all?'

'It hurts a bit when I take a deep breath.'

'OK. I'm going to check your neck and put a collar around it and then I'll listen to your breathing. What's your name?'

'James. Colin James.'

'Have you got any medical problems I should know about, Colin? Do you suffer from any heart conditions? Asthma? High blood pressure?'

By the time the first assistance arrived, Maggie had completed a thorough assessment on both victims and was happy there were no serious injuries. Colin's neck pain was probably due to mild whiplash. The collar was just a precaution until an X-ray examination could confirm her impression. As Maggie introduced herself and handed over the various components of scene control, she found herself becoming the centre of attention rather than her patients.

The ambulance arrived after the fire service and police and the crews of those vehicles were ready for the approach of the young, male ambulance officer.

'Watch out, Jason,' they warned jovially. 'Your boss has beaten you to it. This is Maggie Johnston, the new station manager for Lakeview.'

'You're kidding!' The officer's face split into a wide grin. 'Welcome to Central Otago, Maggie.'

'Hell of an introduction.' Maggie returned the grin. 'I'm not supposed to start work till Monday.' She was surprised but not at all put off by her future colleague's short, dread-locked hair. He looked intelligent and had a very friendly smile. She held out her hand. 'But thanks for the welcome.'

Her hand was shaken warmly. 'I'm Jason Locke. I got your update from Control on the way so I knew there was someone here who knew what they were doing. Has the status changed for either patient?'

'No. Mrs James was uninjured. Neither were KO'd and both have a GCS of 15. Colin has two out of ten neck pain, no associated neurology. He's got some bruising from the seat belt but his chest is clear. Abdomen's also clear. Blood pressure is 130 over 90. He's got a minor laceration on his right forearm which I've dressed. That will probably need a few stitches. I've put a C-collar on and made a note of baseline vitals on both patients.'

'Cool.' Jason was nodding. Then he grinned again. 'You wouldn't like to complete the paperwork while you're at it, would you?'

Maggie raised an eyebrow. 'Are you single-crewed?'

'That's nothing unusual at the moment. We've got plenty of staff for the patient transfer side of the service and they're qualified to fill gaps in the emergency roster, along with the volunteers, but we've been pushing them a bit hard for the last couple of months so it's not just me that's been looking forward to your arrival.'

'What would you like me to do?'

'I'll grab a backboard,' Jason said. 'If you could help with the extrication and another assessment before I head off I'd be very grateful.'

Maggie also completed the two patient report forms and

offered to travel with the ambulance if someone else could drive her car.

'If it was a serious injury I'd take you up on that offer,' Jason said. 'But we're fine, now. One of the fire guys, Andy, is a mate. He'll drive me back. I'm sure you'll want to get into town and get settled before it gets any later. Or colder. Call in at the station tomorrow and I'll give you the grand tour.'

'Thanks. I suppose I'd better try and find where I'm staying before it gets dark. The address sounds a bit isolated.'

'Where are you heading?'

'I need to look for a turn-off about six kilometres past the hospital. I take Spencer Road and then head off on an unnamed road across the paddocks looking for a house by the lake. I'm told I can't miss it.'

'Sounds like Doc Patterson's place.'

'It is. He's an old friend.'

'No kidding?' Jason shook his head as he pulled the back doors of the ambulance closed. 'Small world, isn't it? Is that why you've come to work in this area?'

'No.' Maggie's smile was almost rueful. 'It's just a lucky coincidence.'

It *was* a coincidence. Maggie had had no idea that Hugo Patterson had settled near Queenstown when she'd applied for the ambulance station manager's position. And it was lucky in that it was solving a temporary accommodation hassle, but Maggie had doubts about the arrangement. Surely, if Hugo had been happy about it, he would have contacted her himself and not sent a message and directions via their respective mothers. The message had also been unexpectedly welcoming. If Hugo was so keen to see her, why had he not made any contact for more than a decade? And why had Hugo's mother deemed it necessary to give her the information that he was unmarried and in some kind of relationship with a most unsuitable woman? It was none of her business after all. Maybe she was heading into a situation she would regret.

She couldn't regret her impulsive decision to try a new start in a totally new part of the country, however. Maggie completed the last few kilometres of her journey towards Queenstown completely awed by the magnificent surroundings. Some of the Southern Alps' most impressive peaks towered over the deep, glacier-gouged lakes in the area and Wakatipu, the huge and icy-cold serpent-shaped lake she was approaching now was the most famous. Reading up on her destination recently, Maggie had been intrigued to learn that the lake 'breathed' with a rhythmical rise and fall of its water level every five minutes. Maori legend had the lake being formed when an evil, sleeping giant had been set on fire, melting the snow and ice of the nearby mountains to fill the eighty-kilometre-long lake. That the movements were caused by variations in atmospheric pressure was an explanation of far less appeal.

Hugo lived right on the shore of the breathing lake and Maggie suspected that he would present the scientific version of the peculiar phenomenon. Not that Hugo was unimaginative or stuffy, but he had always been a fount of knowledge, and old and wise enough to be completely trustworthy. He had been more than a big brother figure. Hugo Patterson had been the only man of any significance in Maggie's early life and she had loved him as much as his sister Felicity had.

Far enough removed in years to have seemed always adult, Hugo had been there whenever it had mattered. He'd helped with child care, homework and transport. He'd put up with the girls' teasing, ignored the minor pranks and applied appropriate justice when needed for the major ones. In retrospect, Maggie knew he'd been fair in repri-manding her more than Felicity on most occasions and she'd accepted those judgements eventually. She knew that an undercurrent of strong affection had tempered any dis-approval and the fact that she had returned his affection had made the agonies of puppy fat, pimples, braces on her teeth and that appalling hair all the harder to bear.

Yes, his affection had been returned. And more. But Maggie had never admitted to that teenage crush, even to Felicity, and it had been easy to hide once Hugo had been away at medical school. Felicity's death had finally sev-ered their connection and the estrangement had hurt. The ultimate judgement had been that she had been in some way to blame for the tragedy and Maggie had been dev-astated enough to accept it without ever having the courage to challenge more than her own interpretation.

Maybe Hugo's invitation to stay was an indication that the past was finally behind them. That they could both find the closure that had been somehow elusive despite the pas-sage of so much time. The notion was welcome but it was also rather nerve-racking and Maggie freely admitted to herself that she *was* nervous. What she wasn't prepared to admit was that part of the nervousness had nothing to do with having to relive past traumas. Maggie was drawn to this reunion for reasons she would never try to analyse too deeply.

It could be disguised as mere curiosity. The only photo she had of Hugo was nearly fifteen years old. Had age dimmed the strong lines of his face? Faded the rich dark brown of his hair? Had he gone bald perhaps and started wearing spectacles? And what kind of man was Hugo now? Maggie's memories had built him into a yardstick by which all other men had eventually failed to measure up. What if she'd wasted the last ten years looking for a replica of someone who didn't actually exist?

Nervousness was not an emotion that Maggie tolerated for long. Action overcame fear and Maggie had never lacked the confidence to take action. These days she had learned to think a little more carefully about consequences, however, and she was optimistic that she had made a good choice in coming to Central Otago. That she was going to see Hugo and possibly renew an old friendship was a bonus. She was looking forward to the responsibilities and challenges in taking up the job she loved passionately in a new and exciting place.

So new that Maggie had no idea where she was going and missed the turn-off at Frankton. Taking advantage of the error, she carried on into the township of Queenstown, promising herself a cup of good coffee after making the prudent purchase of a more detailed map of the area. The lack of any discernible twilight was disconcerting, as was the darkness when she finally doubled back along the main road, but Maggie simply gave herself a mental shake. She was going to have to be able to locate obscure addresses in the area at night soon enough. At least this would be a practice run without a potentially life-threatening emergency waiting at the other end.

The hospital complex was easy enough to spot and Maggie noted the ambulance station on site. She didn't slow down for a better look, however. Hugo had probably been expecting her to arrive well before this and she didn't want to add to any nuisance value her visit might already have caused. Spencer Road was also easy enough to find but driving over the rough shingle road that led off to the right felt like a venture into the totally unknown.

The darkness was a blanket, the empty spaces of paddocks on either side vaguely threatening, and the silence when Maggie stepped out of the car to open a wire gate was oppressive. This was the back of beyond, and somewhere at the end of this road lay a lake that housed a sleeping giant and a dwelling that housed a man that Maggie was suddenly almost frightened of seeing again.

'Sorry I'm late. Something smells fantastic.'

'It smelt a lot better half an hour ago.' Joan accepted Hugo's brief kiss and the bottle of wine he was holding. 'Mmm. A white Burgundy. That'll go perfectly with the fish. Or what's left of it.'

'Sorry,' Hugo repeated. 'I got held up. There was an MVA up the Cromwell gorge.'

'Oh.' Joan's murmur was understanding, now. 'How bad was it?'

'Nothing serious. We just had to exclude a cervical fracture by X-ray. Bit of minor suturing. We discharged them both.'

'I heard the sirens.' Joan lived in the tiny settlement of Frankton, between the hospital and Queenstown. 'But that was hours ago.'

'It took a while to tidy everything up,' Hugo responded. 'You know what those cases can be like. Then I had to duck home for a bit.' Hugo sat down on a cream leather sofa with a relaxed sigh. Joan's apartment, a small unit in a complex overlooking the holiday camp, was a space that Hugo was now quite familiar with. Not as relaxing as being at home but pleasant, nonetheless. Not that he was given much time to unwind. He had to stand up again almost immediately as Joan placed a steaming platter on the dining table.

'We may as well eat this before it dries out any more.'

The continued reminder of being later than he had forecast was irritating. So was the 'please explain' expression on Joan's face.

'Why did you have to go home?'

'I was expecting a visitor. I thought she might have arrived and found the house locked up.'

'She?'

'Maggie.' Hugo watched as Joan served a portion of what looked like an exotic mix of steamed trout and herbs. 'She wasn't there so I just left the house unlocked and a note telling her to make herself at home. I said I had an important date I didn't want to miss.' Hopefully, sharing the inspired if somewhat inaccurate content of the note would improve Joan's uncharacteristically reserved mood.

Joan added little bundles of carrot slivers and green beans tied up in some kind of plant material to their plates and then sat down.

'Who's Maggie?'

'An old family friend. My mother asked me to put her up for a few days.'

'Oh.' Joan's smile reappeared. 'She's a friend of your mother's, then?'

'Not exactly.' Hugo tasted the fish. 'This is great,' he enthused. 'What are those little green things?'

'Capers.'

'Taste bombs, aren't they?' Hugo took another mouthful. 'Wish I could cook like you do.'

Joan was extracting bones from her fish with surgical precision. 'What do you mean by "not exactly"?'

Hugo repressed a sigh. 'Maggie is like a kid sister, I guess. She was my sister Felicity's best mate. They were like twins growing up.'

'I didn't know you had a sister.'

'I don't.' This time the sigh escaped. 'Not any more. She was killed in a car accident when she was nineteen.'

'Oh…I'm so sorry, Hugh. I didn't know.'

'No,' Hugo agreed sombrely. 'Of course you didn't. I never talk about her.'

The silence grew and had the effect of highlighting the distance suddenly apparent between them. Why had Hugo never spoken of such a personal catastrophe? Joan glanced at him several times before speaking again.

'It'll be nice to see her again, then. Maggie, I mean,' she finished awkwardly.

'I'm not sure about that,' Hugo said slowly. Maybe it was time to be more open with Joan. The friendship had ticked along at a snail's pace for so long now. Maybe it was time to test the waters and see if it was ever going to come to anything really meaningful. Time to give more of himself than he'd ever been prepared to with any woman.

'Actually,' he said quietly, 'I haven't seen Maggie since she and Felicity headed off to Europe when they were eighteen. That's twelve years ago.'

'And the accident happened overseas?'

'In Greece.' Hugo nodded. 'They were in a van and it got hit by a bus and rolled over a cliff.'

'And Maggie was driving?'

'No.' Hugo raised an eyebrow. 'What makes you think that?'

Joan frowned. 'I just got the impression that maybe you blame Maggie for the accident and that's why you're not so keen to see her again.'

'Maybe I do,' Hugo admitted. 'Felicity should have been off to university when she finished school. She was very bright and she had a passion for history which was what she intended to major in. Taking a year off to go traipsing around Europe seemed like a waste of time. It was Maggie's idea, of course.'

'Why of course?'

'Because it was always Maggie who had the ideas. Felicity was only too happy to trail in her wake. Anything Maggie thought of doing was wildly exciting but she would never have gone to Europe by herself. She never had that kind of confidence.'

'And has Maggie never even made contact with you since the accident?' Joan sounded horrified. 'Surely she realised how devastating it must have been for you?'

'She was pretty devastated herself.' Hugo had known at the time that keeping his distance had been harsh but it had been the only way he could possibly have coped. 'She was quite badly hurt in the accident herself so she couldn't travel back for the funeral. She wrote a couple of times but I never got round to answering and months turned into years and I suppose neither of us would have wanted to revisit that part of our lives.'

'So why did you offer to let her stay with you?'

'I didn't. My mother offered on my behalf.' Hugo shook his head as he smiled. 'She's another woman who can be rather persuasive.' He took a deep breath. 'But never mind. I'm sure I can cope with seeing Maggie. I moved on from all that a long time ago.' Hugo's smile was for Joan this time. 'That's probably why I never bothered mentioning it to you.'

'I'm glad you have,' Joan told him. 'So I guess it's a good thing that you're getting this visitor. Let's just hope she's not intending to stay for too long.' She reached for the silver serving spoon. 'Would you like some more of this trout? It's not so bad after all, is it?'

The house was softly lit. Warm, inviting and…empty. Well, almost empty. Maggie grinned at the three dogs who were circling her feet, sniffing suspiciously.

'It's OK, guys. I'm not a burglar and I've got permission, see?' She waved the note she had taken down from the front door. 'This says I can make myself at home, the blue bedroom's mine, there's soup on the stove and you lot don't bite.' She held out her hand to one of the rangy black and white dogs, who backed away warily.

Maggie smiled ruefully. 'I hope your owner's a bit friendlier than you are. Or is he the one who bites?'

Pretending she was not miffed by the wall of canine suspicion, Maggie quickly explored the house. The main room was not huge but it felt spacious due to its open-plan design, leading at one end to the kitchen and dining area and opening to a television den at the other end. French doors to the verandah were draped against the chill of the night but Maggie could imagine the view on an early summer's morning, watching the sun rise over the lake. The bedrooms also had French doors opening to the long verandah and Maggie had already spotted the casual wicker furniture on the wide outdoor extension to the house. Service areas, including two bathrooms and a laundry, were on the side of the house away from the lake but basically the dwelling was single-room width, built on the lake's edge like a holiday cottage.

It seemed ancient. The wide, wooden floorboards had the rich patina of age and matched hardwood beams latticed the plaster ceilings of most of the rooms. The bathrooms and kitchen were up to date, however, and the old coal range that was keeping some delicious-smelling soup hot looked as though it had been kept purely for its aesthetic value. Furnishings appeared to have been chosen for comfort rather than style and the huge leather chair beside the woodburner looked as inviting as the soup smelt.

Maggie was tired. She had started the long drive down from the ferry terminal at Picton yesterday and had stopped overnight in Christchurch. She thought she'd paced the journey well but the interruption of dealing with that accident had drained any remaining energy. She pulled only the bare essentials of her possessions from her car to put in the spare bedroom with the pale, blue walls and darker blue bed covering, and then went to explore more thoroughly what the kitchen had to offer. A loaf of bread topped a wooden board beside the stove and Maggie helped herself to a thick slice, breaking off a piece of crust to nibble as she hunted for a suitable mug to ladle soup into. She noticed the eyes then. Four of them, with another two lurking a little further back. She grinned.

'Oh…I'm not so bad now that I'm holding food, is that the story?'

A tail thumped. Then another. Maggie could have sworn the dogs exchanged vaguely embarrassed glances before sidling closer. Maggie held out what was left of the crust. 'So, who's going to be brave enough to go first, then?'

She hoped Hugo wasn't a big eater. If he'd intended that loaf of bread for his breakfast he might be annoyed to find that Maggie had shared so much of it with his pets as she'd bribed them into friendship.

'Mind you, we don't have to tell him, do we?' Maggie put the empty soup mug down on top of the pile of medical journals covering the table beside the chair. She curled her legs up so that she could lean more comfortably into the lovely old leather cushions. She scratched the set of ears that stood out from the rest by having one black and one white. The dog closed its eyes wearily.

'Come on, then.' Maggie drew her legs into a tighter ball and patted the space she had created on the chair beside her. 'You look like you need a rest as much as I do.'

It was later than Hugo had intended by the time he headed home but he hadn't expected to have to spend his evening making amends. He still wasn't quite sure what he had been trying to atone for. His lateness, initially, but then what? Not Joan's suspicions about him having a female house guest. He had no reason to feel guilty about that. It was more likely to have been the revelation of how little they really knew each other that had made him feel so guilty.

Hugo suspected he had spent the last three hours or so trying to do something about his lack of involvement in the relationship. Trying to let Joan know that he hadn't been simply stringing her along for reasons of personal convenience. He had even kissed her with more enthusiasm than usual, too, but the lack of any overwhelming ambition to take her to bed still hadn't changed. It had been Joan who had decreed that they take things slowly but a year was a bit ridiculous in anyone's book, wasn't it? And why hadn't he felt inspired to do something about it?

He was too tired to worry about it now and it was irritating to feel like he had something else he would need to make amends for when he went into his own home. Maggie had probably felt unwelcome, arriving to an empty house with an impersonal note taped to the door. But she wasn't welcome, was she? Maggie Johnston carried with her too many reminders of things Hugo had done his best to move on from. The thought of stirring parts of his soul best left to lie in peace was disturbing. It had been tough enough telling Joan the bare facts. Hugo realised then that that was the reason he had spent so long in Joan's company tonight. He would have denied it strongly but he had been nervous about going home.

What was he going to find? A Mack truck filling the woolshed? An older but still stroppy female who might make demands on the strength of their past association?

Trouble had always followed Maggie like a boisterous puppy, ready to leap unexpectedly and over-enthusiastically into prominence but never causing major damage. At least, not until that ill-fated trip overseas. Hugo shook his head. There was no point revisiting any of that again until he had to.

And maybe Maggie had changed. There was no vast truck parked in his woolshed. Just a very ordinary, small Toyota hatchback. And his house looked perfectly peaceful. Quiet. Too quiet, maybe. Where were the dogs? Had Maggie given up waiting for him to come home and taken herself off to bed? Hugo let himself into the house carefully so as not to disturb his guest if she was asleep. He clicked the front door shut quietly and trod softly across the short hallway to enter the living room. Then, two steps into the room, he stopped.

Maggie *was* asleep. Curled up in his big, leather chair. Two dogs lay guarding her feet, including Tuck—the dog who accepted no stranger but now had his nose resting on the chair's cushion. And Lass, who was so shy it had taken Hugo weeks to win her trust, was actually *on* the chair with Maggie, coiled into a ball that fitted neatly behind Maggie's knees. The gaze she bestowed on Hugo was frankly guilty and the white-tipped tail waved apologetically.

It was the movement of the dog that woke Maggie. She blinked in confusion for a long moment as Hugo stared back at her but then her face came alive, the smile extending to a delighted grin as she scrambled to her feet, scattering reluctant dogs.

'*Hugo!*'

And with the sound of her voice myriad memories rushed at him. He could hear two voices. Young girls of about eight or nine. Teasing him as he arrived home from school.

'Hugo!'

'No, *you* go!'

'No! *Hugo*!'

He could hear the echo of giggles but he could also remember the welcome that had lain beneath the teasing. Who else had ever been that pleased to see him? Had lain in wait to tease him unmercifully but had also sought him out to share something new and exciting or seek assistance when, once again, they had landed themselves in some kind of trouble?

Only Maggie and Felicity, that was who. And now it was just Maggie, but the pleasure of seeing him was there in her eyes and it was just the same. Hugo had to breathe in past the painful constriction his throat was experiencing.

'Oh, Maggie,' he said quietly. 'It's so good to see you again.' And to his astonishment, he found the words were true.

He held out his arms and then, to his consternation, Maggie's grin faded and gold-flecked hazel eyes sparkled with gathering tears. But then Maggie was in his arms and Hugo was being hugged with breathtaking enthusiasm and he was aware of nothing but the feeling that a huge chunk of his life that he had believed had gone for ever had just— miraculously—been given back to him.

CHAPTER THREE

'SHE'S gorgeous.'

'Hmm.' Hugo was trying not to allow his attention to waver but it was proving difficult.

'What did you say her name was?'

'Maggie Johnston.' Hugo raised his gaze from the patient file on the desk in front of him with a small sigh.

'And she's a paramedic?'

'That's right.' Hugo found himself smiling as he remembered Maggie's delight in discovering that he had expected her to arrive driving a truck.

'It was probably *my* mother's fault that she got it wrong. She still calls me an ambulance driver despite me explaining in great detail that ambulance *officers* actually do a lot more than just drive.' Hugo had forgotten that half thoughtful, half mischievous gleam that Maggie's eyes were so good at producing. 'I wouldn't mind trying a big truck one day, mind you. Could be fun!'

Maggie was having fun now by the sound of it. Unfortunately, the area used to wash ambulances down was right outside the window of the office that Hugo and his companion, visiting cardiology specialist Donald Hamilton, were using. Maggie had just missed soaking Jason Locke with the high-pressure hose she was holding. Probably intentionally, judging by her shriek of laughter as Jason threatened to retaliate with a soggy mop.

Donald was grinning now, or was it more of a leer? 'Looks like she's having fun.'

'Maggie always has fun.' Hugo was unaware of his proprietorial tone or the faint edge of envy. Why was it that he had never discovered that happy knack of fitting in so well and so instantly somewhere new? Of making friends that easily? Of finding things, no matter how trivial, to be amused by? He'd never been distracted from a consultation before by people who were enjoying a chore like cleaning a vehicle, for heaven's sake.

'Does she now?' Donald's expression was definitely in the leer category now and his obvious interest in Maggie was suddenly irritating. Hugo cleared his throat.

'Charlie Barker,' he reminded Donald somewhat curtly.

'Ah…yes. I saw him today, didn't I? Nice chap.'

'Seventy-two-year-old,' Hugo nodded. 'Triple vessel disease. First infarct three years ago.' He opened the file. 'I think you did his cardiac catheter investigation and the angioplasty yourself.'

Donald glanced at the report, a map of the major arteries of the heart with shaded segments showing the abnormalities discovered and treated. 'Yep. The LAD and circumflex were quite markedly narrowed, although the infarct was relatively minor.' He turned a page. 'Three stents altogether. I ballooned this segment on the right coronary as well. He did very well. Almost normal cardiac output and he was pain-free on follow-up for…let's see…' Pages fluttered as Donald looked for the outpatient clinic notes.

'He was free of angina for eighteen months,' Hugo agreed. Charlie had, in fact, had a great year after recovering from the scare the heart attack had given him. One of Hugo's first patients after starting work in the area, the semi-retired builder had quickly become a favourite. When Hugo had bought his property, Charlie had insisted on helping him plan and then carry out his conversion of the old shearers' quarters. He had come to know Charlie, and his wife Betty, very well over the course of that year and he was very fond of them both. After nearly fifty years together, the couple were still virtually inseparable and the Barkers confirmed Hugo's faith that marriage could be a wonderful institution if you were lucky enough to find the right person.

'His blood pressure's under good control. The lipid profile still looks good and the rhythm's stable.'

'His angina isn't. He's getting pain more often with less provocation and the GTN is less effective.'

'He's on the waiting list for bypass surgery.'

'He's been on the list for nearly two years now. His condition's deteriorating.'

'I know.' Donald sighed wearily. 'And I'm sorry but there's not much I can do about that. The waiting list keeps growing. Every time we get another acute patient it cuts the numbers we can take from the list. It's an ongoing battle. We're doing our best to increase funding so we can put more cases through. Can he afford to go private?'

'No.'

'I'll put his score up and see if we can move him up the list. I can't promise anything, though, Hugo. You know that.'

Hugo nodded. Both men were silent for a moment and Donald's gaze travelled back to the window. The ambulance was moving back into the garage now but Hugo knew the cardiologist's attention had returned to one of its crew. He closed Charlie's file.

'Have you got time for a coffee before your flight back to Dunedin?'

Donald checked his watch. 'No. I'd better head back across the road to the airport.'

'I'll walk over with you.' Hugo stood up as well. 'I could do with some fresh air.'

An opportunity to put in another plug on Charlie

Barker's behalf would also be welcome but Hugo was distracted by the route Donald chose. Had it been intentional to pass so close to the ambulance station garage? The glance he gave Hugo as their path coincided with that of Maggie and Jason confirmed that the opportunity had definitely been on Donald's agenda. Hugo found himself forced to oblige by providing introductions.

'Maggie? This is Donald Hamilton, one of our visiting specialists. He's a cardiologist from Dunedin. Donald, meet Maggie Johnston, our new paramedic.'

'Hi.' Maggie's smile was genuinely friendly and she didn't hesitate in holding her hand out to be shaken. Hugo's eyes narrowed slightly. Had it been Donald's idea to extend the handshake quite that long? And did he have to look at Maggie with such blatant admiration? He took a look at Dr Hamilton from an entirely new perspective. The cardiologist was probably in his early forties. Far too old for Maggie.

'Nice to see a new face around here,' Donald was saying warmly. 'How are you enjoying Central?'

'I've only been here for a few days,' Maggie responded. 'This was my first day at work, in fact, but I love it so far. How often do you get here?'

'Once a month, officially.' Donald's tone suggested it was not nearly often enough. 'I try and get down for a long weekend occasionally as well and luckily Queenstown is a popular venue for conferences and suchlike.'

'I'm not surprised. There's so much to do here. It's going to take me years to try everything that's on offer.'

Donald was smiling. 'You sound adventurous, Maggie.'

'You only live once,' Maggie responded with a quick grin. 'Life's supposed to be fun, isn't it?'

'Oh, indeed it is.' Donald's own smile broadened noticeably. He looked set to continue the conversation but Maggie's attention was already elsewhere.

'I'd better go. I've got a mountain of paperwork before I can go home. What time will you be leaving, Hugh?'

'Any time you're ready.' Hugo was quite aware of the speculative glance Donald shot in his direction. He almost enjoyed the assumption the cardiologist was clearly making. 'I just want to check on Nancy and make sure she's still doing well and then I'll be finished.'

It was no surprise that Donald waited only until they had moved on a few paces before seeking clarification.

'I thought you and Joan Pringle were…?'

'Yes.' Hugo didn't expand on his confirmation. He might have a professional relationship with Donald but they were hardly more than acquaintances. 'We are.'

'But you're taking Maggie home?' Donald's eyebrows rose. 'Lucky man.'

The innuendo was unexpectedly grating. Hugo disliked what it suggested about Maggie as much as any slur on his own morality. 'Maggie's staying with me at the moment because she's an old family friend. I've known her since she was two years old.'

'Really? How old is she now?'

'Thirty.'

'And she's not married, is she? She's not wearing a ring, anyway.'

'She's not married.'

'Attached?'

'Not that I know of.' They hadn't discussed their love lives at all. Maggie had clearly known about Joan's existence before she'd arrived and Hugo hadn't tried asking Maggie any such personal questions. There had been quite enough to discuss just catching up with their professional lives over the last decade. Maggie's nursing background, as well as their common interest in emergency medicine, had provided a wealth of conversational material. So had Hugo's quick guided tour of Maggie's new location over the weekend. So far, by tacit agreement, they had not delved too deeply into their shared past. It had to come, of course, but right now Hugo was happy to renew their friendship and simply enjoy Maggie's company.

He was less happy with Donald Hamilton's company right now but he'd be able to leave him at the airport terminal in less than a minute.

'How long will she be staying with you?'

'As long as it takes her to find a place of her own, I guess.' Hugo pitched his tone to suggest it was none of Donald's business. He had been a little more forthcoming in fielding a similar question from Joan earlier that day, but it had been annoying nonetheless.

'That won't be easy at this time of year.' Donald stopped just short of triggering the automatic doors of the small airport terminal.

'There's no rush.' As far as Hugo was concerned, Maggie could stay as long as she liked, even if Joan did disapprove.

'Indeed.'

Hugo had had enough of this conversation. 'How's your wife, Donald? And the kids?'

'Don't see much of them these days, old chap. We've split up.'

'I'm sorry to hear that.'

'These things happen.'

'Indeed.' Hugo unconsciously echoed Donald's speech mannerism, and his light tone belied the faintly disturbing possibilities the information conveyed. He pushed his hair away from his eyes as he took his leave and strode back towards the hospital complex. He had no idea he was frowning quite so heavily until he passed Joan in the corridor.

'Goodness, Hugh. What's up?'

'Nothing. Why?'

'You look as though you're on your way to tear strips off someone. Not me, I hope?'

'Of course not.' The thought of Joan ever doing something that might require a severe reprimand was amusing and Hugo smiled.

'Was that Donald Hamilton I saw you talking to outside?'

'Yes.' Hugo shook his head. 'He's taken quite a shine to Maggie.'

'Really?' Joan's tone suggested surprise rather than disapproval. Then she frowned. 'I thought he was married.'

'Apparently not any more.'

'Oh.' Joan's glance slid sideways. 'That's all right, then.'

'I suppose so.' Hugo pushed his hair back again and Joan smiled.

'Looks like you're due for a haircut.'

'Hmm.' Hugo tried to listen to Joan but his mind was not co-operating. What was it to him if Donald Hamilton and Maggie got together, anyway? It was high time he shook off any vestiges of the umbrella of responsibility he had assumed during Maggie's adolescence. Felicity's well-being had been his primary concern after all. Maggie was free to do whatever she wanted with her life, with whomever she wanted to do it with. She did not need and would probably not welcome any brotherly advice from him.

'So, seven o'clock, then?'

'Sorry?'

'Friday.' Joan frowned just enough to cause a tiny

crease to appear between those pale blue eyes. 'Dinner? At your place?'

'Ah.' It was his turn again, then. Hugo nodded as though he had been listening all along but then changed the nod into an apologetic shake. 'Sorry, Joan. There's a group going out on Friday night. The ambos are having a welcome dinner for Maggie and some of the GPs and nurses are going along. I said I'd go. Lizzie and Megan are both going, I think.' Hugo smiled at Joan. 'I assumed you'd been invited as well.'

'I was.' Joan's lips looked thinner than they had a moment ago. 'I said I already had a date.'

'Well, why don't we both go? It might be fun.'

'Hmm.' The sound was an echo of Hugo's lack of interest in discussing the length of his hair. Then she shrugged. 'Why not? It's about time I met the woman you're living with, I suppose.'

'I'm not *living* with her,' Hugo said patiently.

It wasn't Maggie's fault that she chose that moment to bounce into view in the corridor. She was smiling broadly.

'Time we went home, Hugh. Don't know about you but I'm *starving*!' Maggie was still smiling as she slowed down. 'Hi…you must be Joan.'

Hugo hid his surprise. How on earth had Maggie known that? Joan, however, looked mollified that Maggie clearly knew who she was.

'That's right.' She moved a little closer to Hugh. 'I'm Joan Pringle.'

'Maggie Johnston.' The hand was extended with the same enthusiasm Donald Hamilton had received but the handshake was considerably more brief. Hugo was disconcerted to see that gleam in Maggie's eyes again. Thoughtful. And downright mischievous. At least Joan wouldn't recognise it or realise its potential. Hugo stepped in hurriedly.

'Time we went. We need to get that tyre changed on your car so you've got your own transport tomorrow. I'll be at the medical centre in Queenstown and I'll have house calls in the afternoon so I'd be completely unreliable as a taxi.'

'I doubt you've ever been completely unreliable in your whole life, Hugh.' Maggie's smile took away any hint of criticism in the comment but Hugo was still wary of that gleam. He was relieved when the women said goodbye and Maggie kept up as he walked briskly towards the car park.

'So...' Hugo gave Maggie a sideways glance. 'How did you know about Joan?'

'Your mother told me,' Maggie said innocently. Too innocently.

Hugo was suspicious. 'What else did she say?'

'Not much.' Maggie avoided meeting Hugo's gaze. She could see instantly why Joan was unsuitable. She had a handshake that felt like picking up a dead fish. Maggie hid the beginnings of a smile. There was something fishy about her eyes as well. She had to wonder how serious the relationship was and her embryonic smile faded as she decided that Hugo might, in fact, think Joan Pringle was eminently suitable.

Hugo had followed the play of emotions on Maggie's face that ended with almost a frown. 'Joan's a lovely person.' It was annoying to hear the defensive note in his voice and he tried to modify his tone. 'Talented, too.' He pointed at the wall as they crossed the reception area. 'That watercolour is one of hers.'

'Mmm.' Maggie sounded impressed. 'She can certainly paint. What else does she do?'

'She's an excellent nurse and a qualified midwife. She's great with kids and she's an absolutely fabulous cook.'

'Wow!' This time Maggie couldn't suppress the grin. 'Sounds like perfect wife material.'

Hugo scowled. 'If my mother's put you up to pushing me into producing grandchildren in the near future, forget it. I'll do what I want *when* I want.'

'Good for you,' Maggie said mildly. 'I can relate to that.' She climbed into the Jeep. 'Are we going to get take-aways again tonight?'

'No, I'm cooking. I've eaten out more this weekend than I usually do in a month.'

'Thanks so much for showing me around. I hope Joan didn't mind not seeing you over the weekend.'

'She was in Dunedin, visiting her mother.' Hugo wasn't about to admit that the routine of Friday night dates was only broken when work commitments interfered and that, so far, they'd never spent a weekend in each other's company. Somehow, in Maggie's presence, a strictly adhered-to routine seemed embarrassingly boring. At least he was planning to try cooking something adventurous this evening. With a bit of luck, Maggie might not discover how unusual that was.

For some inexplicable reason, the fish didn't look anything like the dish Joan had produced last week despite Hugo's attempt to follow the recipe faithfully. Capers sat, looking like decomposed peas, on the rather watery and pale trout flesh. Maggie didn't seem to mind, however. They took their plates over to the circle of warmth from the fire and Hugo ordered Tuck and Lass off the small sofa opposite his leather chair so Maggie had somewhere to sit.

'Great salad,' Maggie enthused. 'Love the dressing.'

'Thanks.' The dressing had come from a bottle. Hugo found himself glancing up at intervals to try and catch

Maggie's expression when she took a mouthful of the fish. Would she find it as horrible as he did? The expression he caught clearly had nothing to do with his cooking, however. It seemed disconcertingly personal.

'Why are you staring at my hair?'

'Damien would love it.'

Hugo forgot any worry about what Maggie would think of the fish. 'Who the hell is Damien?'

Maggie grinned. 'The hairdresser I found in the East End of London. I fell in love with him two minutes after I walked through the door.'

Hugo forced another forkful of fish down as he raised an eloquent eyebrow to indicate that such an inappropriate reaction didn't really surprise him. Maggie's grin simply widened.

'Not that Damien was remotely interested in *me*. He was outrageously camp. Limp wrist, lisp—the lot. He took one look at my hair and nearly fainted.' Maggie's expression changed dramatically. She put down her fork, laid the back of a limp wrist against her forehead and gave a despairing cry. 'My God, thweetie,' she moaned. 'Haven't you heard of *product*?'

The take-off was entertaining enough to make Hugo laugh out loud. He hardly noticed the next mouthful of fish. Maggie sighed happily.

'He gave me hair. *Real* hair. You've got no idea what a life-changing event that was.'

'Why?'

Maggie's eyes widened with disbelief. 'Don't you remember what my hair was like?'

'Um…' Hugo thought back. He remembered the snub nose. The freckles, the braces on her teeth and, yes…the hair. 'It was red,' he said triumphantly. 'And kind of…frizzy.'

'It wasn't *hair*,' Maggie corrected him darkly. 'If I cut it short I looked like a toilet brush. If I tried growing it, it went sideways so I looked like I'd stuck my finger in a live socket.'

'It doesn't look like that now.' Hugo let his gaze rest admiringly on the fascinating cascade of auburn spirals that just touched Maggie's shoulders at the front and lengthened to hang between her shoulder blades at the back. The urge to pick a spiral up and wind the curves around his finger took Hugo by complete surprise. He cleared his throat. 'It looks…OK.'

He turned his attention back to his meal. It didn't look OK. It was gorgeous hair. Different. Barely tamed, with the potential to leap back to a wild and uncontrollable state. A bit like Maggie, really. No wonder Donald Hamilton had been smitten.

Maggie's lips twitched. 'Thanks,' she said drily. 'I like it, anyway.'

They ate in silence for a minute and then Hugo frowned. 'So why would Damien love my hair? It's as straight as it comes.' His eyes narrowed suspiciously. 'I suppose he'd want to perm it and give me a few "curlth".'

Maggie giggled but shook her head. 'There's product to cure anything. A bit of wax or fudge and you could stop it flopping into your face like it does. Don't you get sick of shoving it out of your eyes?'

'Of course. I missed my haircut last week because of an emergency. I just haven't found time to slot another appointment in yet. It doesn't flop if it's short enough.'

'Oh, don't cut it,' Maggie said in horror. 'You'd lose those lovely blond streaks. Or are they grey?' The gleam was there in full force now. Her hazel eyes sparkled with it. 'And you should make the most of your hair while you've got it. Let's see, you must be…thirty-six now?'

Hugo nodded, his mouth too full of the last horrible bite of fish to say anything.

'There you go, then. You'll probably start going bald soon.'

Hugo swallowed. 'Cheers.'

Maggie grinned, completely unabashed. 'I've got something in my bag that might do the trick. Why don't you give it a go?'

'I've managed for thirty-six years without smearing goop in my hair. Why should I start now?'

Maggie's eyebrows shot up. 'Why *not*? You might find you like it. Sometimes trying something new can be a life-changing event.'

'I like my life just the way it is.'

'OK.' Maggie was still unperturbed. 'I'll leave it in the bathroom, though, in case you change your mind. It's a little orange jar.' She stood up, holding an empty plate and walked towards the fridge. 'I don't suppose you've got any chocolate ice cream in there?'

'No. Ice cream's unhealthy.'

'It's therapeutic in small doses,' Maggie said firmly. 'Like many medications. You should know that, being a doctor.' Her face brightened. 'Never mind. I'll put it on the shopping list.'

'You'll have to wait till Thursday, then. That's the day I do my grocery shopping.'

'I'll make my own list,' Maggie decided. 'I'm not here to sponge off you. I'm extremely grateful to have a roof over my head but I'll make my contribution to the groceries while I'm here and I'll share the cooking. It'll be my turn tomorrow.' Maggie didn't give Hugo time to protest. 'What do you like? Curries? Sushi? Nachos?'

'Ah…' Hugo blinked. 'Not sushi. I'm not really into seaweed.' In fact, he'd just decided he'd gone off fish.

Good for Maggie, he thought abstractedly, eating his effort without a murmur of complaint. 'Even in small doses,' he added hurriedly. 'I do know it's supposed to be good for you. I'd prefer something hot anyway.'

'Great. I know exactly what to make in that case.'

Water was not going to do the trick. Hugo could feel beads of perspiration gathering in astonishing places.

'What is *in* this?'

'Chilli.' Maggie used a corn chip to scoop up a large dollop of the rich meat, bean and tomato mix on her plate. She caught a string of grilled cheese and used her fingers to wrap it around the laden chip. 'Mmm.' It was a moment before she could speak again. 'You did say you wanted something hot for dinner.'

'I meant temperature, not something that was going to remove the entire lining of my digestive system.'

'Chilli's good for you,' Maggie said knowledgeably. 'It speeds up your metabolism so you burn off more calories.' She grinned. 'I consider this a diet food.'

'"Die" being the operative syllable,' Hugo groaned. He refilled his water glass.

'Sorry. I didn't realise you weren't used to a bit of spice in your life.' Maggie leapt to her feet. 'What you need is yoghurt, not water. I've put some in the fridge.'

Hugo took the proffered pot and spoon reluctantly. Yoghurt was something else that never made an appearance on his menus. At least it wasn't likely to inflict physical damage. In fact, the cooling effect was quite impressive.

'Hey! It works.'

'I learned that one in India.' Maggie nodded. 'When I tried my first local vindaloo.' Her brow creased. 'You don't have to eat the rest if it's too hot. I could make you something else.'

'No, I like it.' Hugo was surprised to realise the polite statement was actually sincere. 'It tastes great. It's just a bit fiery.'

'I'll tone down the chilli next time,' Maggie promised. Her face was deceptively composed. 'And I'll be careful when I make you vindaloo.'

'Thanks.' Hugo took a more cautious amount of the meat mixture on his next chip. 'So. How was your day today?'

'Fantastic. I'm starting to learn where things are on station and how it all works. We took the four-wheel-drive vehicle up to Coronet Peak to get a skier with a broken leg. We didn't get to go up in the chair lift, though.' Maggie's face creased with disappointment. 'The mountain rescue team had already retrieved him and the doctor in the first-aid room had splinted the fracture and given him pain relief.' She looked disgruntled now. 'We were just a taxi service really. We delivered him to the fixed-wing aircraft for transfer to Invercargill.'

'The ski slopes are pretty well covered for emergencies,' Hugo nodded. 'You'll find a lot of people in the township use the twenty-four-hour emergency cover the medical centre provides as well.'

'Do you do nights there as well?'

'No. I'm employed by the hospital apart from Tuesdays when I have a day at the medical centre. When I'm not needed for medical duties I deal with the administrative side of things. I'm on call at nights for the hospital from Monday to Friday as well. Not that I get called in very often.'

'I'm beginning to suspect I won't get called very often either.' Maggie shook her head as she smiled. 'But, then,

I knew I was heading for a quieter workload. I've had enough of big-city dramas and feeling exhausted by the end of every shift. The idea of working business hours and still having plenty of time out on the road was very appealing. And there's lot of other things I can do here.'

'Like what?'

'Like training for the volunteer staff here and in the more remote areas. Improving some of the procedures and updating equipment. I think we can streamline our transfer service to take patients to Invercargill or Dunedin and that will give more people the opportunity to spend time with the emergency side of the service.'

'Won't the administrative stuff get boring? I find it a bit much at times.'

'I'm hoping I'll still get a reasonable case load to keep life interesting. Plus, I've done helicopter work before so I'll be available to go out with the chopper crew they contract for rescue work here. That way they won't have to wait for a GP to come out from the medical centre.' Maggie gave Hugo an anxious glance. 'They won't mind, will they? I don't want to start treading on toes by taking away an exciting part of their duties.'

'I certainly won't mind. It's incredibly disruptive to get called for a helicopter job.' Hugo grimaced. 'Not to mention downright scary.'

'Scary can be good,' Maggie said. 'It keeps life exciting.'

'Life doesn't have to be exciting to be good,' Hugo countered.

The unspoken reminder of the repercussions of seeking adventure in the past hung between them in a moment of silence. Was Hugo going to take the opportunity to talk about Felicity? Maggie wondered nervously. She poked the food on her plate, her appetite suddenly gone. Hugo's tone was sombre when he spoke but his words did not invite any conflict.

'Safe can be pretty satisfying as well.' The glance Maggie received was unreadable. 'Isn't it about time you grew out of being so adventurous?'

Maggie's smile was tentative. 'You sound like my mother.'

'And mine,' Hugo had to admit ruefully.

'And I am settling down,' Maggie added softly. 'I've come here, haven't I? I'm going to try a more peaceful lifestyle.'

'Hmm.' Hugo was unconvinced. 'That remains to be seen, doesn't it?' The look in his eyes was one Maggie remembered well. Stern but affectionate. She held his gaze as she smiled back at him.

'Watch this space.'

CHAPTER FOUR

MAYBE safe *would* be satisfying after all.

The helicopter was flying low due to the bank of cloud threatening to dump a fluffy new layer of snow onto the peaks towering behind them. Maggie could see the ripples on the lake beneath, caused by the current the helicopter rotors generated, and she could almost make out the startled expressions on faces peering from the deck of the old steamship below. Maggie leaned forward in her seat to snatch another glimpse of the vessel.

'What a cool boat!'

'That's the TSS *Earnslaw*.' The voice of Graham Burgess, the pilot, crackled through the headphones built into Maggie's helmet. 'She's been steaming around Lake Wakatipu for more than seventy years. Does a nice dinner cruise.'

'I'll put that on my list.' Maggie sat back and tried to relax, letting the safety belt she was wearing take her weight as the helicopter turned sharply and left the flat expanse of the lake behind. The ride became rougher, which seemed appropriate given the wild terrain they were now flying over. And it would probably get worse.

'What's the weather going to do?'

'Should hold for an hour or so.'

'That's good.'

Maggie succeeded in hiding her nervousness. She hadn't worked with this crew before. Or in the kind of untamed wilderness offered by the bush-covered slopes beneath them. It had been a long time since she'd done any heli-

61

copter work at all, especially a winch job. Why had she remembered the adrenaline rush and excitement of such work and forgotten how mind-blowingly scary it could also be?

And why had she been so eager to make her qualifications known to the team who manned the helicopter service when needed? The fact that her duties had been comparatively light for the first couple of weeks wasn't really enough of a reason. Mind you, talking to the crew hadn't prepared her for having her first call-out so soon and the excitement of having a break in a day of mostly administrative duties had worn off now.

'It's lucky we've got you in the area.' The co-pilot, Sam, must have caught the direction Maggie's thoughts had taken. 'We haven't had anyone trained in winch procedures until now. With the city choppers unavailable, this guy would have had to be stretchered out to a landing site and, by the sound of it, he wouldn't have lasted that long.'

'It doesn't sound good,' Maggie agreed. The call was for a gunshot wound to the chest, and the potential injuries had been ticking over in the back of her mind ever since she had been contacted. It was difficult to know what she'd be facing. A direct wound to any major arteries near the heart would have killed the victim swiftly. Lung tissue was relatively tolerant of a projectile injury but rib fractures with an associated pneumothorax would be high on her list of suspicions. A lot depended on whether the victim had been breathing in or out when the bullet had struck. If a bullet entered the lower chest during exhalation when the diaphragm was relaxed it was quite likely to cause an abdominal injury. Her patient could be bleeding out through a major injury to his liver or spleen. Whatever the possibilities, it was highly likely to be serious. Maggie shook her head slightly.

'How often do deer hunters fail to identify their targets and shoot each other instead?'

'Too often,' Sam grunted. 'Especially with the international, recreational hunters that get choppered into remote areas. They've got no experience of terrain like this and common sense goes out the window with the prospect of scoring a stag.'

Maggie's common sense was gathering with disturbing strength as the helicopter dropped and then tipped, following the precipitous mountain face. The spray from a spectacular waterfall billowed towards them. She had to be crazy, doing things like this for a living.

'That's the Homer tunnel to our right,' Graham informed Maggie.

Maggie spotted the narrow snake of road disappearing into the side of a mountain and then she looked up again. She had already lost count of the waterfalls, with their white foam brilliant against the dark grey of the rock faces and the deep green of the bush enveloping the slopes.

'And this is the head of the Milford Sound coming up,' Sam pointed out a short time later. 'Been here before?'

'No.'

'It's supposed to be the eighth wonder of the world.'

Maggie simply nodded. The water of the sea beneath was so dark it appeared black. With the mountains crowding in to the sides and, above them, the impenetrable-looking bush and the glowering bank of cloud as a ceiling, the overall effect was awe-inspiring but vaguely threatening. The helicopter was slowing now and losing height as it turned towards a valley.

'We're heading north again, now, into the Pembroke Wilderness area. Should reach our target in a minute or two.'

'Roger.' Maggie took a very deep breath. Sam was a

trained winch operator and Graham a pilot of many years' experience. It was time to step into her role as a helicopter paramedic and do this job without being distracted by any fears for her personal safety. It was an easy role to assume as they closed in on a target area that had been relayed with reasonable accuracy. The flare the victim's companions had been instructed to set off pinpointed the area of bush-covered slope even more precisely.

'Target sighted.' Graham sounded satisfied. 'Three hundred metres, nine o'clock. Turning downwind.'

'Roger.' Sam was peering through the Perspex panel of the side door. 'I see them.'

Maggie paused in her task of checking the contents of the trauma pack. She strained to catch sight of the target but could see nothing but the canopy of trees. Sam was reaching for the winch control panel.

'Checking power,' he advised.

'Turning base leg,' Graham responded.

Maggie shut her eyes for a split second. These guys knew what they were doing.

'Final two hundred metres to run.'

'Roger.'

'Speed back. Clear door,' Graham instructed.

Sam pushed the door open as the helicopter slowed again. 'Door back and locked,' he announced. 'Hook coming in.'

There was no time to think of anything other than adhering strictly to procedure now. Maggie clutched the large hook and fumbled a little as she attached it to her harness.

'Check your pit pin,' Sam ordered. 'And then release your safety belt.'

'One fifty metres,' Graham told them.

'Ready, Maggie?' Sam's gaze was steady but Maggie could detect an underlying concern. Her ability to do this job was as untested for them as their skills were for her. She could put them all in considerable danger if she wasn't competent. Her nod was decisive and Sam's face relaxed fractionally. 'Moving to door,' he said tersely. 'Clear skids.'

Maggie moved carefully, turning to face into the helicopter as she found her footing on the narrow skids. Sam faced in the opposite direction, leaning out to keep the target in sight. 'Eighty metres,' he reported. 'Seventy… Clear to boom out.'

'Clear,' the pilot advised.

Maggie stepped off the relative safety of the skids. Her stomach lurched as the harness took her weight and her legs dangled in the air. Sam attached the lightweight stretcher and the trauma pack to an extension on the winch hook.

'Booming out,' Sam said calmly. He was still calculating the distance to the target. 'Minus forty…thirty-five… Clear to winch out.'

'Clear.'

Maggie was staring down as she steadied the stretcher and pack between her legs. The trees were too close together for comfort but there was enough space for a talented pilot and winch operator to get her safely to the ground provided the weather conditions co-operated. The helicopter was hovering now and Maggie was unperturbed by the fact she was now spinning in a slow circle herself.

'I'll keep you clear of the trees.' Sam's voice came through her helmet clearly as she felt herself being lowered. 'What's your distance, Maggie?'

Her legs had just gone below the level of surrounding treetops. 'Forty feet or so,' she told Sam. She kept watching, concentrating on the ground coming up to meet her rather than the tree branches reaching out to try and snag her cable. 'Minus twenty,' she said, seconds later. 'Fifteen…ten, nine, eight…'

Her descent slowed and Maggie was impressed by the controlled touchdown Sam gave her.

'Weight's coming off,' she heard him relay to Graham.

Maggie unhooked the clips holding herself and the gear. She held the hook well clear of her body, now aware of her audience at ground level. Fortunately the two men were standing at a safe distance. After a hand signal to Sam, the hook moved up and away swiftly. Then the helicopter gained height, ready to hover as it waited for her to complete her part of the operation. The mixture of anxiety and relief on the faces turned towards Maggie made her all the more aware of her responsibility in this mission.

'You take the stretcher,' she shouted at the men over the noise from the climbing helicopter. 'I'll take my pack. Where is he?'

'Just in the trees over here. Pete's with him, keeping pressure on the wound to try and stop the bleeding.'

'It's bad,' the other man warned. He looked at Maggie as though he hadn't expected to see anyone of her age or sex arriving to try and save his mate. 'Are you going to be able to help him?'

Maggie was already moving. 'I'm certainly going to do my best.'

'So, how bad was he?' Hugo was leaning forward in his leather chair, one hand resting on the head of the dog leaning against his legs. 'And how did you start your assessment?'

'He wasn't in good shape.' Maggie pulled her legs up onto the couch and leaned back. It was so good to be able to wind down finally. It was even better to relive the buzz the day had provided by sharing it with such an interested listener. 'GCS of 7, responsive only to painful stimuli. His airway was patent but he was tachypnoeic with a respiration rate of 36. No radial pulse. Carotid was weak and he had a tachycardia of 130.'

'Pretty shocked, then. What was his blood pressure?'

'Seventy-five over 40 but I didn't get that initially. I got some oxygen on and then cut his clothes to have a look at his chest.' Maggie grinned wryly. 'That was a job in itself. Have you got any idea how many layers a deer hunter has to wear in the middle of winter?'

'I can imagine.' Actually, Hugo was having a hard job trying to imagine Maggie out there in the wild, fighting alone to save the life of a severely injured man. She'd been winched in from the chopper, for heaven's sake! The idea of Maggie facing the kind of dangers such a feat presented gave Hugo an oddly mixed reaction of astonishment that she was capable of such work, admiration in hearing her sound as though she was as skilled as she was capable and sheer disapproval of her putting herself into such a risky situation. Admiration was winning hands down at present.

'The entry wound was left-sided and quite low. It had fractured some ribs and left enough of a hole to bleed profusely but I suspect the lung damage was relatively minor and the bullet carried on to make a hole in the liver or spleen. Or both. The abdomen was pretty tense.'

'Did you put more than one IV line in for fluids?'

'Yes, but the second one was *en route*.' Maggie grimaced. 'It was lucky it wasn't an arterial stab with the air pocket we hit.' She caught Hugo's questioning gaze. 'I got a 16 gauge in on the ground and got one of the guys to squeeze a litre of saline in fast but that wasn't before I dealt with the sucking chest wound.'

Hugo whistled softly. 'Pneumothorax?'

'Yep. It tensioned within the first couple of minutes I was on scene. It was lucky we got there when we did.'

'What did you do?'

'Covered the open wound with an occlusive dressing and did a needle decompression.'

Hugo shook his head. 'You make it sound easy.' He knew perfectly well how tense an emergency like that could be within the controlled environment of an A and E department. How much worse would it be as the sole medical officer, in a hostile environment, with limited supplies and equipment? His glance was frankly admiring. 'How long did you spend on scene?'

'Twelve minutes,' Maggie said proudly. She was enjoying the new experience of impressing Hugo Patterson but she didn't want to take all the credit. 'I was glad of the other men being there. That made getting him into the stretcher and winched up much faster. And Graham and Sam were just brilliant. They're a great crew.'

'Did you take him to Dunedin?'

Maggie nodded. 'He was as stable as we could hope to get him. What he needed was to get to Theatre as quickly as possible.' Her smile was delighted. 'We made it, too. He's going to survive by the sound of it.'

'Well done.' Perversely, Hugo felt envious of the way Maggie had spent her afternoon. 'I had a day full of toddlers with ear infections and old people with their chronic airways disease exacerbated by upper respiratory tract infections.'

'Maybe you should do some winch training,' Maggie suggested. 'Then you could go instead of me next time.'

'I could think of a lot of things I'd rather do,' Hugo said drily. He eyed Maggie curiously. 'Weren't you scared at *all*?'

'Terrified,' Maggie admitted cheerfully. 'But only briefly.

Once you start thinking about your patient instead of your-self, it goes away. And I guess the danger is what makes it so exciting,' she added. 'Especially when it's a difficult job and you get a successful result.'

'And you said you were coming here for a quieter life,' Hugo sighed. 'What is it with you, Maggie Johnston? Are you going to keep flinging yourself into dangerous situations until your walking frame gets in the way?'

'Oh, no.' Maggie closed her eyes and rested her head on the back of the couch. 'I'll retire from any really active duty when I get pregnant.'

Hugo's jaw dropped. 'You're planning to get *pregnant*?'

Maggie's eyes opened again. 'Of course. I've always wanted to have kids some time.'

'When…precisely?' Hugo still sounded horrified.

Maggie grinned. 'Don't worry, I'm not planning on solo parenthood. I'll wait until I find a suitable husband.'

'So you haven't got anyone in particular in mind?'

'No.' Maggie sighed sadly. 'I thought I had a while back but it fizzled.'

'Why was that?'

'He was a bit older than me. Drop-dead gorgeous but…' Maggie chewed her bottom lip thoughtfully. 'He turned out to be drop-dead boring as well. No adventure in his soul.' Maggie sighed again. 'It was a shame but I guess you can't have everything.'

'No. I guess not.' Hugo felt some sympathy for the nameless hunk. How hard would it be to impress Maggie with having an adventurous soul? Good grief, it would be hard enough just keeping up with her, let alone providing any kind of exciting challenge. Hugo couldn't even con-template attempting such a feat. His speculative gaze was met by a glance from Maggie which, despite her obvious weariness, contained that unique, mischievous gleam.

'I'm not in a huge hurry to find anyone else,' she told him reassuringly. 'I'm quite enjoying being a virgin.'

Hugo was stunned into silence. This was way too much information and he didn't believe a word of it, anyway. Nobody who looked like Maggie could have successfully fended off the approaches men must have been making for at least the last ten years.

Maggie giggled at his expression. 'I guess you don't read the right magazines,' she said kindly.

'No,' Hugo agreed wryly. 'Closest thing I get to a magazine is a medical journal.' And the only publications Joan ever had lying around for him to flick through were of the *House and Garden* or *Gourmet Cuisine* variety.

'I doubt that this theory has hit *The Lancet*.' Maggie chuckled. 'But according to the article I read, if you haven't had sex for more than a year you become a virgin again. Born again, so to speak.'

Hugo cleared his throat. He knew he was being teased. The turn in this conversation reminded him a little too clearly of the way both Maggie and Felicity used to see how far they could wind him up by embarrassing him with details of feminine issues. And he found himself reacting in the same old way. Trying to retreat and keep his dignity intact.

'It's late,' he announced stiffly. 'I'm going to give the dogs a bit of fresh air and then head off to bed.'

'I'll come with you.' Maggie scrambled off the couch. 'I still need to wind down a bit before I'll sleep. A walk on the beach is just what I need.'

'Get your coat, then,' Hugo ordered. 'And a hat. It's starting to snow.'

'OK, Dad.' Maggie shot him a cheeky grin as she pulled a woollen hat down over her curls.

The dogs had woken and were circling Maggie's legs.

Hugo turned to check that the woodburner's door was safely closed and then he smiled at the scene waiting by the front door. Maggie looked as eager as the dogs for the brief outing before bedtime. Despite the impressive account of her day's activities and the somewhat shocking reference to her sex life, she was still just a kid. The thought of her even wanting to have children of her own seemed incongruous but Hugo realised with a jolt that she was the same age as Joan. All grown up. Maggie could easily have produced several children by now if she'd wanted to.

Hugo followed the small troop as they headed out into the freezing darkness, the dogs and Maggie apparently equally excited by the light swirl of snowflakes dancing in the beam from the torch Hugo held. The shingle crunched beneath his boots as they reached the beach and he found himself smiling again. Maggie couldn't be considered exactly restful company but he wouldn't want her any other way, would he? If she was different, she wouldn't be Maggie. And he was glad she hadn't found someone she wanted to have children with. If she had, she wouldn't be here with him now, making him shake his head but laugh with increasing frequency.

A small corner of his brain suggested that he was pleased she hadn't had sex with anyone for more than a year as well, but Hugo damped that thought down hurriedly. He didn't want to know and he certainly wasn't going to try and analyse why the information had been pleasing.

It snowed all night and the amount that settled on the ground meant there was no way Maggie's little car was going to cope with the roads next morning.

'I'll take you in the Jeep,' Hugo offered. 'I'm in at the hospital all day today.'

The dawn was gathering momentum as they drove through paddocks softly blanketed with a startlingly white cover. The headlights of the Jeep made it sparkle alluringly but Maggie's gaze was directed upwards, waiting and watching as the pink glow over the mountain peaks blossomed. Hugo stole a glance at her face. And then another. Her eyes had a brilliance that competed with the flashes of colour from the snow and her lips were parted slightly in wonder.

'I just don't believe it,' she said softly a minute later. 'This must be *the* most beautiful place in the world.'

'It is lovely,' Hugo agreed, but he broke his concentration on the road for only a moment to appreciate the sunrise. The view a little closer was also lovely. Disconcertingly so. He could never have anticipated that Maggie would have turned into such an astonishingly beautiful woman. The realisation that he could find her attractive hit him like a brick.

This was *Maggie* sitting beside him, for heaven's sake. He had known the girl for ever, and the feelings he'd always had for her alternated between protectiveness and annoyance overlying a genuine fondness. It couldn't have been termed a friendship. The difference in their ages had precluded a relationship on the kind of equal terms friendship required, but that would have come in time if it hadn't been for the accident. The reminder of the still unexplored shadow in their past was enough to push Hugo's errant thoughts into perspective.

Sure, Maggie was an attractive woman. And maybe now they had the opportunity to forge the friendship that had been denied, but that was all that could ever come from renewing their acquaintance. And it was all Maggie could possibly want. She'd called him 'Dad' last night when he'd reminded her to put some protective clothing on. She still saw him as part of a generation removed from her own. Safe. Restrictive, probably. And boring. He didn't have any ambition to go on jaunts in a helicopter, did he? Or even to read popular women's magazines.

Joan Pringle was much more to Hugo's preference when it came to women. Collected and confident but not overly so. She sought reassurance about everything—a new hair-style or outfit, her handling of patients and, most especially, her painting. She was looking a little apprehensive later that day when Hugo was escorting another visiting consultant to the outpatient department. Joan was adjusting the level of a new framed canvas on the wall of the corridor.

'Stand over there for a second, could you, please, Hugh? Is it straight, do you think?'

'Looks fine.' Hugo eyed the picture. 'Better than fine. It's terrific.'

Joan's gaze slid to his companion. 'What do *you* think, Lewis?'

'I like it.' The respiratory physician took his time admiring the picture. 'That's the *Kingston Flyer*, isn't it? That old steam train that does the tourist run around the lake?'

Joan nodded. 'I thought it was a nice way to show the perspective of the Remarkables in the background.'

Hugo mirrored Lewis's nod. 'It's great. Even without the train it would still be lovely with the lake and mountains. You've captured the feel of the landscape beautifully, Joan.'

'You didn't paint this, did you?'

Joan was basking in Lewis Evans's disbelieving stare. 'Yes, I did.'

'But it's fantastic! You're very talented.'

'Thank you.' Joan glanced at Hugo who smiled his agreement.

'There's a few more gracing our walls,' he told Lewis. 'You must have seen the ones up in the outpatient department.'

'Yes, but I had no idea who'd painted them.' Lewis turned to Joan. 'Do you sell any?'

'I've never tried.'

'Do you *want* to sell any?'

Joan was blushing now, with charming modesty. 'I really don't think they're *that* good.'

'I beg to differ,' Lewis said firmly. 'And I have a friend with a gallery in Dunedin whom I'm sure would agree with me. Maybe we should book you in for an exhibition.'

Joan's gaze was fastened on Hugo. 'What do *you* think, Hugh?'

'I think you should go for it,' Hugo said promptly. 'If that's what you want to do.'

Joan looked even more apprehensive. 'But what if people hate them?'

'They won't.' Hugo and Lewis spoke at the same time.

'Think about it,' Lewis added. 'Why don't you lend me one of your paintings and I'll show it to my friend and give you a ring next week? I'll be down every fortnight over the winter anyway. We're getting into peak season for respiratory problems.'

'Mmm.' Hugo was reminded of the direction they were supposed to be moving in. 'There's a heavy clinic for this afternoon and we've got another two people we want to get onto a home oxygen supply. I've got their files in my office.'

'Let's go and have a look before clinic starts.' Lewis

paused only long enough to smile warmly at Joan. 'Don't forget to think about that exhibition, will you?'

Joan didn't forget. It was still uppermost on her mind when Hugo took her out to dinner on Friday night.

'I'm really nervous about it,' she confessed.

'You need to have more confidence,' Hugo told her. Maggie would never agonise over something like this. She'd throw caution to the wind, enjoy any success and simply laugh off any adverse reactions or put them down to experience. It was the kind of attitude that simplified life. Try anything and make the most of the good bits.

'Being confident of one's own abilities can come across as showing off.' Was Joan following Hugo's train of thought? 'You should have heard Maggie in the staffroom yesterday, talking about that accident victim they had to cut out of the car that rolled off the Remarkables' access road.'

'It was a tough job,' Hugo said mildly. 'They were working in sub-zero conditions on a patient with serious head and spinal injuries. Getting him stable enough to fly out was a real achievement.'

'You would have thought she'd done the intubation and everything else herself, the way she was talking.'

'She did.' Hugo shouldn't have taken such pleasure in Joan's astonishment but he actually felt proud of the way Maggie had handled that job. 'Maggie's an advanced paramedic. She has a range of emergency procedures and drugs she can give that make me feel quite redundant. There's not much more I can do in A and E that she can't do out on the road. In fact, she gets far more practice getting IV access or intubating than I do these days.'

Joan's shrug was infinitesimal. 'It'd be nice if she looked a bit more professional, then. Why doesn't she tie her hair up properly?'

Hugo grinned. 'She reckons there hasn't been a hair tie invented that can cope with her curls.' He liked the way she dragged the front pieces back to anchor the spirals that hung between her shoulder blades. When she was in her uniform of crisp white shirt and epaulettes, dark trousers and steel-capped black boots, she looked every inch the professional in his opinion. Not that the shirt was always so white when she came off duty, mind you. 'And what about young Jason?' he added. 'You've never complained about his dreadlocks.'

'That's different.' Joan was staring at Hugo with an odd expression. 'Come to think of it, your hair looks a bit…different.'

'I just haven't got round to having it cut.'

'So why isn't it falling in your face like it usually does?'

Hugo felt vaguely embarrassed. 'It's fudge,' he muttered.

'Sorry?'

'Goopy stuff. I wouldn't have tried it but Maggie leaves all her stuff lying around in the bathroom and I kept knocking it off the shelf when I picked up my razor, so I decided to give it a go.'

'Sounds messy.' Hugo wasn't sure if Joan was referring to the product or Maggie, but it became clear a moment later. 'Hasn't she found somewhere else to live yet, Hugh? She's been at your place for three weeks. People are starting to talk.'

'Let them,' Hugo said airily. Joan's eyes widened reprovingly but he just shrugged. 'There's nothing to talk *about*,' he added firmly. 'And it's my business who lives in my house.'

Joan was silent for long enough to let Hugo know that it was also her business.

'She's been looking,' he assured her. 'She thought she'd

found a perfect house last week and then learned they wanted six hundred dollars a week for it. Even with flat-mates, it's more than she could possibly afford.'

'There's a unit in my complex that may be coming vacant. I could talk to the landlord.'

'Hmm.' Hugo couldn't sound enthusiastic. He thought of the way Maggie headed outdoors with the dogs at every opportunity, no matter what the weather was like. She'd tramp over the paddocks and up the hills or along the beach and come back with glowing cheeks and eyes and wild hair that was begging for extra product. He couldn't imagine her shut up in a shoebox apartment like Joan's. 'Why don't you talk to Maggie about it?' he suggested.

'I'll do that.' Joan pushed her unfinished dessert to one side. 'If I get the chance to get a word in edgeways some time.' Her glance at Hugo was very brief. 'She loves to talk, doesn't she?'

'Sure does,' he agreed. 'It will probably drive me nuts before long.'

Joan smiled. 'She'll probably drive us all nuts. Except Lizzie. Ever since that night out with the ambulance staff she seems to have adopted Maggie like a long-lost daughter. And Megan,' Joan added after a pause. 'She thinks Maggie's wonderful.'

Hugo just smiled. 'She's always made friends easily. I remember the whole of her kindergarten class trailing home with her one day. She'd let them all out the gate when the teachers were dealing with some emergency in the loos. I came home from school to find three police cars parked next door.'

Joan rolled her eyes. 'I can't believe the way everyone's gone overboard on her idea for the hospital fundraiser. I was sure the committee would vote for the craft fair or concert.'

Hugo had to agree with Joan on that one. 'Can't say I'm looking forward to a fancy-dress ball either. It's not my idea of a fun night out.'

'Nor mine,' Joan said fervently. She smiled at Hugo. 'Are you ready to go, Hugh? I've sorted out a few paintings at home. I'd really appreciate your opinion on whether I should include them in an exhibition.'

'Actually, I really need to pop into the hospital,' Hugo said apologetically. 'Nancy's been a bit off-colour again today and I want to check on her before leaving her for the weekend.'

'I could come with you,' Joan offered. 'And wait.'

'I'll have to get home pretty soon. Maggie went out somewhere tonight and the dogs will need attention.'

'Oh? Where did she go?'

'I'm not sure. I suspect it has something to do with Donald Hamilton having a weekend in Queenstown.'

'You don't sound as though you approve.'

'He's far too old for her.'

'He's only in his forties. Hardly geriatric.' Joan was playing with the spoon still resting in her dessert plate. 'Lewis Evans is about the same age as Donald and *he's* still an attractive man.'

Was that a challenge or was Joan just annoyed by his interest in Maggie's social life? Hugo had the sinking feeling that he was getting himself into trouble here. Even without the constant references to Maggie that seemed to have peppered their conversation he was putting a patient and even his dogs' needs ahead of Joan's. She might well think he was making excuses not to go back to her apartment and Hugo felt a stab of guilt because he suspected there was an element of truth in that. He tried to sound a little more enthusiastic.

'Maybe I could come back long enough for a coffee and to look at those paintings.'

'That would be nice.' If Joan was upset at the prospect of Hugo not staying longer, he couldn't detect it. Maybe she'd never been that keen to break down the barrier that kept them as friends rather than lovers. Those hints about advancing age and having babies might have been generic and not intended as some kind of ultimatum. Hugo hoped so. Joan was a pleasant companion, a good friend and probably—as Maggie had suggested—perfect wife material, but Hugo had no intention of stepping onto that path just yet.

Any attraction to the prospect of a permanent relationship with Joan had, in fact, diminished somewhat over the last few weeks but Hugo was at a loss to know precisely why. He hadn't changed. Joan certainly hadn't changed. Consistency was one of her attributes after all. He knew that Joan hadn't exactly warmed to Maggie but that was hardly surprising, given their diverse personalities. The disapproval of him having Maggie as a house guest might have something to do with the new atmosphere but Hugo wasn't going to jump through that hoop. If Joan wanted more than friendship she'd have to trust him, wouldn't she? Having a female house guest who was the equivalent of a younger sister shouldn't be enough of a problem to have thrown up a new barrier.

But something had. And Hugo had an uncomfortable feeling that he didn't want to try and summon the amount of enthusiasm it would take to break through that barrier.

CHAPTER FIVE

'Is my nose as red as it feels?'

Hugo looked up from where he was towelling off one of the dogs after their Saturday morning outing on the beach the next day. 'Yep.'

'I think I've got frostbite. It's even hard to smile.' Maggie bared her teeth at Tuck who was stoically waiting for her to finish drying his feet. The old dog stretched his neck and licked her squarely on the lips. 'Oh…yuck!' Maggie used the corner of the soggy towel to scrub at her face.

'That's hygienic.' Hugo grinned. 'I think I would have stuck with the dog lick.'

'I need a shower anyway.' Maggie straightened from her crouch. 'And a roaring fire. And some soup. I'm *so* cold.'

'At least it's stopped snowing. It might be a good afternoon to take the chair lift up Coronet Peak. The view is amazing and you haven't done that ride yet.' Hugo held the door to the living area open and the three dogs headed gratefully for the warmth of the fire. 'Or…if you prefer to stay warm, we could do the gondola thing and have some hot chocolate in the restaurant at the top.'

'I'm sure you've got better things to do with your afternoon than taking me sightseeing.'

Hugo appeared to give the statement serious consideration. 'Sadly, no.'

'Why sadly?'

'Because telling you that my idea of a perfect winter afternoon is sitting by the fire catching up on some journals might just confirm your opinion of how boring my life is. How boring *I* am, in fact.'

'Oh, you're not boring, Hugh,' Maggie assured him. She hung her jacket up and then pulled the woollen cap off her head, releasing tendrils of hair that spiralled gleefully into disarray. 'Safe, yes, but never boring.'

'So you won't try and make me try bungy-jumping or extreme skiing if we go somewhere this afternoon?'

'Perish the thought.' Maggie raised an eyebrow. '*Can* you ski?'

'Not very well,' Hugo admitted. 'Can you?'

'Haven't really tried,' Maggie said. Her eyes gleamed. 'Yet. I guess that's a whole new adventure waiting for me. Hey, I could sign up for some lessons if we go up to the ski field.' The gleam intensified. 'I wonder if I can find some hunky Swedish ski instructor who'd take me on?'

Hugo closed his eyes as he shook his head sorrowfully. He had no doubt at all that any available male would be happy to take Maggie on, given half a chance. 'Wasn't your date with Donald Hamilton exciting enough, then?'

'It wasn't a *date*.' Maggie was in front of the woodburner now. She crouched to open the door. 'I think he just wanted company for dinner. There's a conference on this weekend and he arrived early. I declined to go to the cocktail session they had later. I was home well before you,' she reminded Hugo. She poked another log into the burner and her lips twitched mischievously. 'I guess Joan has exciting depths to her personality that I have yet to discover.'

'I wouldn't know.' Hugo was astonished at himself for making such an admission. 'At this point in time we're just good friends.'

Maggie rocked back on her heels. 'Don't tell me you're a born-again virgin, too?'

'I have no intention of telling you any such thing,' Hugo said grimly. 'Mainly because it's none of your business.'

'Sorry.' Maggie bit her lip. She was horrified at having asked but it had just popped out. And now she was dead curious. According to the hints Joan dropped at frequent intervals, she and Hugo were practically engaged. Maybe she was holding out to make sure she got a ring on her finger. The thought was uncharitable but Maggie wasn't happy with Hugo's choice of woman and the more she saw of Joan Pringle the less happy she became.

If Hugo married someone like Joan, they would both sit around reading on a winter's afternoon. They'd probably have a string of well-behaved blond children who would also keep their little noses buried in books or paint lots of pictures of trains and hills. He might find the idea attractive but it would definitely be the way to step from safe into boring. What Hugo Patterson needed was someone to show him how much fun there was to be had out of life.

Someone like herself.

The thought was far more shocking than her personal question about Hugo's sex life had been. Even in the throes of her teenage crush Maggie had never considered herself a potential partner for Hugo. He was way out of her league. Far older, far more clever and far too good-looking. He was a role model for the man she was looking for, not the man himself. Was it just the intervening years that now made the age gap seem so insignificant? Or made her feel as though they discussed things both professional and personal on an almost equal footing? Maggie could feel the colour creeping back into her face and suspected she could pass for a good imitation of Rudolf the red-nosed reindeer. She'd been firmly put into her place again, hadn't she? It was none of her business.

Hugo noted the embarrassment Maggie was trying to

disguise by stuffing the woodburner with as many logs as she could fit in but, hell, he was just as embarrassed. The very thought of discussing his sex life, or rather the lack of it, with Maggie was decidedly shocking. The silence in the room was just becoming unmistakeably awkward when the telephone rang.

'I'll get it.' Hugo sounded relieved. A moment later, however, he was frowning tensely. 'Try and calm down, Betty. When did his pain come on? Has he used his GTN spray? How many times?' He was still frowning and already dark brown eyes looked almost black with concern. 'He needs to come in to the hospital straight away, Betty.' He listened again. 'Well, that's certainly going to be the quickest way if you think you can manage. We can send an ambulance out if you need it. Tell you what, you start driving and I'll send the ambulance to meet you. That's going to be the fastest. I'll meet you in at the hospital.'

Hugo hung up and found Maggie standing right behind him. 'Someone with chest pain?'

'Charlie Barker. One of my patients.'

'Cardiac history?'

'A long one. Previous MI and on the waiting list for bypass surgery.' Hugo was still holding the telephone. 'I'd better despatch an ambulance.'

'There's only volunteer staff on at the weekend. I'll go.'

'You're not on duty. Why should you go?'

'Because they're not qualified to give him anything more than oxygen or GTN or aspirin. They won't even be able to get an IV line in and if you're looking this worried he probably needs one. How far out of town does Charlie live?'

'About twenty minutes. Past Arrowtown on the way to Wanaka.'

Maggie was already heading for the door. 'What are we

waiting for, then? If he's having an MI, every minute counts, Hugh. Time is muscle, as they say.'

'You're right.' Hugo grabbed his mobile phone and his coat. 'We'll take the Jeep. It'll be faster than your car.'

It took only a few minutes to reach the ambulance station but Maggie used the time to quiz Hugo thoroughly. She wanted to know how old Charlie was, his full medical history, what medications he was on, whether he was allergic to anything and whether this chest pain differed from the angina he usually suffered. Hugo had to interrupt the flow of queries to answer his mobile phone.

'Don't panic, Betty. We're on our way.' He glanced at Maggie. 'She can't find her car keys and Charlie's been sick.'

'How long is it since the pain came on?'

'Just over twenty minutes now.' Hugo slammed the Jeep to a halt and they both leapt out, startling the volunteer ambulance officers sitting inside the station building.

'What's happened?'

'Patient of Hugh's might be having an MI,' Maggie told them. 'I'm just going to grab my paramedic kit and we'll head out to get him. Are the life-pack batteries fully charged?'

'Yes. Do you want us to come with you?' The older woman who spoke looked anxious.

'I think we'll manage,' Hugo told her.

Maggie was heaving her kit into the back of the ambulance. 'You'd better stay in case another job comes in,' she directed. 'We'll call if we need back-up.'

Hugo had to make two attempts to fasten his seat belt as Maggie put her foot flat to the floor. He'd been in an ambulance before with the beacons and siren blazing but he was sure he'd never reached this kind of speed so quickly. And Maggie wasn't even wearing a seat belt!

Hugo opened his mouth, which felt unusually dry, but one look at the intense concentration on Maggie's face made him close it again. This probably wasn't the moment to mention her oversight with the seat belt. She looked as though she knew exactly what she was doing and in the interests of self-preservation Hugo didn't want to distract her.

Passing two long tourist buses, Maggie then aimed for what seemed a narrow gap between a car that hadn't pulled over or slowed noticeably and oncoming traffic that was also being slow to respond to the emergency vehicle's right of way. Hugo shut his eyes as they screamed through the gap. He held his breath as they took a curve in a road bordered by drifts of old, icy snow but Maggie seemed to know exactly how far she could push the speed of the ambulance. They rocketed through the narrow streets of Arrowtown and then speeded up even more.

'I need directions.' Maggie had been totally silent until now.

'Keep going. Over the next hill it'll be the second…no, third turning on the right.'

Maggie switched off the siren as they turned off the main road. She turned off the beacons as they reached the Barkers' driveway.

'No point in scaring anybody,' she murmured. 'Poor old Betty might really think it was an emergency.'

Maggie backed the ambulance swiftly to the back door of the house, which was framing the anxious figure of Mrs Barker. With a graceful economy of movement Maggie was out of the driver's seat and into the back where she unclipped the strap holding the life pack into position.

'What can I bring?' Hugo climbed through into the saloon with far less grace than Maggie had.

'You take this.' Maggie handed him the heavy life pack. 'I'll get my kit and the oxygen.'

Betty Barker's eyebrows rose as Maggie threw the back doors open and jumped lightly to the ground, swivelling to pick up the bulky paramedic kit with one hand and the portable oxygen cylinder with the other.

'This is Maggie Johnston, Betty,' Hugo told her. 'She's our new paramedic.'

'I'm so glad *you're* here, Hugo.'

If Maggie felt at all offended by Betty's preference she showed no sign of it and Hugo deliberately hung back a little, curious to see Maggie in action. After that hair-raising driving experience he was already viewing her with a rather different perspective. This focussed and professional calm she was exuding was an aspect of her personality he wouldn't have guessed even existed.

Their elderly patient was sitting at the kitchen table and looked distressingly like a classic presentation for a heart attack. His face was grey and beads of perspiration stood out on his forehead. Maggie put down her kit and smiled at him as she ripped open the plastic bag containing an oxygen mask.

'Hi,' she said warmly. 'I'm Maggie. I'm a paramedic. You're Mr Barker, aren't you?'

'Charlie.'

'Is it OK if I call you Charlie?' Maggie had uncoiled the plastic tubing and attached it to the cylinder. She twisted the metal handle to open the valve and then the knob to adjust the flow. 'We'll start some oxygen for you, Charlie, and then we'll do something about that pain you're in.' She glanced up at Hugo. 'Can you put the leads on and get an ECG trace?'

'Sure.' Hugo unzipped the pouch and took out a cable that split into three wires with electrodes on their tips. It took him a moment to find the connection port for the cable and switch the machine on, and as he did so he listened to Maggie's rapid but calm questioning of her patient as she took his blood pressure.

'Where is the pain at the moment, Charlie?'

'Right here.' Charlie pressed his hand to his sternum.

'Just in the one place?'

'I can feel it in my left arm. And my jaw.'

'Pain score on a scale of ten, with zero being no pain and ten being the worst you can imagine?'

'Bloody fifteen,' Charlie grunted from beneath the oxygen mask.

'Blood pressure's 140 over 70 and he's bradycardic at 55.' Maggie had her kit open now and was moving impressively fast. A tourniquet went around Charlie's arm to replace the blood-pressure cuff before she scooped out the other items she needed. She ripped open an IV cannula packet, then a luer plug, then a dressing. Maggie drew up a small syringe full of saline as a flush, but she appeared to be keeping an eye on Hugo at the same time.

'The white electrode goes on the right just under the clavicle. Black on the left and red on the left side below umbilical level. You could put that oxygen saturation probe on a finger as well, if you like.'

'Thanks. It's a bit different to the gear I'm used to.' Hugo peeled off the coverings to expose the sticky side of the electrodes and positioned them on Charlie's chest. By the time he had the second in place he noted that Maggie had swabbed a vein on Charlie's forearm and slipped a cannula in. She released the tourniquet, tamponaded the vein just beyond the end of the cannula, attached the luer plug and taped it into place before covering the site with a clear plastic dressing. Her actions were smooth, polished and incredibly efficient.

By the time Hugo had a trace showing on the screen of the life pack, Maggie was snapping the top off a glass phial. She inserted the needle of a syringe and drew up the drug. Then she handed the empty phial to Hugo.

'Morphine, 10 milligrams, expiry date April next year,' he confirmed.

'Thanks. And this one?'

'Metaclopromide, 10 milligrams. Expiry May.'

'Happy for me to administer them?'

'Sure.'

'Hugh tells me you're not allergic to any medications, Charlie? Is that right?'

'Not that I know of.'

'Cool. This first one is to make sure that the morphine doesn't make you feel sick.' Maggie injected the dose of metaclopromide. 'And this should help that pain.' She injected the morphine slowly, keeping her gaze fixed on Charlie's face. 'How's the rhythm looking?' she asked Hugo over her shoulder.

'Sinus bradycardia.'

Maggie turned her head. 'And ST elevation,' she murmured as she caught Hugo's eye. He knew she was as aware as he was that Charlie was in trouble. The evidence that a heart attack was in progress was fairly conclusive and the slow heart rate could easily herald serious complications like a cardiac arrest. Hugo unclipped his mobile phone from his belt and excused himself to make a phone call out of earshot of the Barkers. It took only seconds to request priority transport to get his patient to the cardiac team in Dunedin and he returned to the kitchen to find Maggie busy packing up her gear.

'Have you had an aspirin today, Charlie?'

'Yes, he has.' Betty had been standing, silently watching until now. 'I line up all his pills first thing in the morning beside his orange juice. *And* I make sure he takes them all.' Her smile at her husband was a valiant effort but still distinctly watery. 'Don't I, love?'

'The Gestapo's got nothing on my Betty.' Charlie returned his wife's smile and Maggie could see the reassurance that he was trying to give her.

'I'll grab a stretcher,' she told Hugo quietly. 'Let's get moving, shall we?'

'I can walk,' Charlie protested. 'I'm far too heavy for a slip of a girl like you to carry. And the pain's a lot better now.'

'No way.' Maggie grinned at Charlie. 'I need the exercise. Imagine how floppy my arms would get if all my patients insisted on walking.'

'Need a hand?' Hugo queried.

'No. You keep Charlie company.' Maggie's glance informed Hugo that she wanted their patient's condition monitored carefully. 'Betty, can you throw a couple of things in a bag for Charlie? Pyjamas and a toothbrush and so on?'

'It's all packed,' Betty said. 'I've kept a bag ready in the hot-water closet ever since that first heart attack.'

Maggie wasted no time in bringing a stretcher into the kitchen. She raised the head end and then opened a blanket to cover the mattress. Together, she and Hugo lifted Charlie despite his protests and then Maggie tucked the blanket around him, pulled up the side of the stretcher and clipped the safety belt into place.

'You'll need that,' Hugo said with a smile. 'Wait till you see Maggie's driving, Charlie.'

'I'm sure she's as good at that as everything else,' Betty said stoutly.

Maggie's glance at Hugo was amused as she fitted the hook of the oxygen cylinder onto the back of the stretcher.

'Unplug the life pack for a minute,' she said. 'We'll connect up again once we get Charlie on board.'

It took only a minute to install Charlie in the back of the ambulance, connect his mask to the main oxygen supply and reattach the cardiac monitoring equipment. Betty sat in the back on the spare stretcher, close enough to hold Charlie's hand.

'You happy in the back, Hugh?' Maggie peered into the saloon. 'You're welcome to drive if you want.' There was just a hint of amusement in her bland tone and Hugo's lips twitched. He'd deserved that.

'I'm happy,' he said. 'Let's get going. The helicopter should be well on the way by now so we shouldn't have too long to wait at the airfield.'

Maggie started the engine and eased slowly over the pot holes in the Barker's driveway. She could hear Hugo talking to Charlie.

'We'll have you in the catheter laboratory in Dunedin in no time, Charlie. With a bit of luck they'll be able to slot you in for a bypass while you're up there.' Maggie could hear a smile in his voice. 'I wouldn't have recommended this course of action but it's certainly the most effective way to bump yourself to the top of the waiting list.'

'Hate waiting,' Charlie said. 'Always have.'

Maggie drove fast but without the spine-chilling speed with which she had responded to the call. They had a fifteen-minute wait at the airfield until the rescue helicopter arrived from Dunedin and they used the time to give Charlie another thorough assessment and complete the paperwork. Maggie helped the paramedic crew transfer Charlie to their own stretcher and load him into the chopper. Then she moved back, surprised to find Hugo with his arm around Betty.

'You OK, Betty?'

'I'm worried sick. Is he going to make it through this time, Hugo?'

'He's certainly not going to give in without a good fight,' Hugo said with a gentle smile. 'And he's going to the best place possible.' He pulled Betty closer and gave her a warm hug. 'Hang in there and ring me later to let me know what's happening.'

'I'll do that.' Betty pulled away from Hugo's embrace. 'Thanks, Hugo…for everything.' The older woman sniffed hard as she noticed Maggie standing beside them. 'Thanks to you as well, dear, for taking such good care of Charlie. I think we're lucky to have you here.'

'They're ready for you now, Betty.' Maggie smiled her acknowledgment of the thanks. 'I'll take you over to the helicopter.'

Betty hesitated. 'I hate flying,' she confessed. 'If it wasn't my Charlie in there, you wouldn't get me near one of those contraptions.'

'It's quite safe,' Maggie assured her. 'I do it all the time.' She took Betty's arm and held her hand. 'Come on. I'll introduce you to the paramedics. They're very nice boys and they'll take good care of you *and* Charlie.'

Maggie and Hugo stood together to watch the helicopter take off. 'I'd like to have gone with them,' Hugo said as the noise from the rotors diminished. 'Shame they didn't have the room for an extra.'

'He's in good hands,' Maggie responded. 'And you would have only been sitting and waiting at the other end.'

'I could have kept Betty company.' Hugo led the way as they moved back to the ambulance. 'She'll worry herself sick until it's all over. It'll be Charlie who keeps it together despite being scared silly himself.'

Maggie drove the short distance to the ambulance station and then climbed into the passenger seat of Hugo's Jeep. 'Are you that fond of all your patients?' she asked curiously.

'Of course not. The Barkers are a bit special.'

'Why's that?'

'I guess I just know them better than most of my patients. Charlie helped me convert what was a pretty rough shed for shearing gangs into my house. It took us about a year and Betty was never far away. She'd sit there with her knitting on nice days and turn up with hot soup and scones on cold ones. They hate being away from each other for too long despite the fact they've been married for more than fifty years.'

'That's so sweet.'

'So unusual.' Hugo turned off the main road. 'Just goes to show how important it is to choose the right partner, doesn't it? Or maybe it's just luck. You wouldn't think it would have been such a successful marriage. They're like chalk and cheese, those two.'

'Opposites attract.'

'Yes, but they don't always find it works out long term. Betty frets and Charlie reassures her. Charlie's always been a real go-getter and Betty's toned him down and kept him out of trouble.'

Maggie made a face. 'I'd hate that.'

'What?'

'Somebody trying to tone me down.'

'Hmm.' Hugo eyed Maggie thoughtfully. 'I guess that's why the hunk had to go.'

'The what?'

'The drop-dead boring guy.'

'Oh, Brian. Yep, he was definitely into toning down. He would have had kittens if I'd ever driven him on a priority-one call-out in an ambulance.'

Hugo felt another twinge of sympathy for Maggie's discarded suitor. 'I have to confess I wasn't exactly at my most relaxed on the way to the Barkers.'

'Calculated risk,' Maggie said lightly. 'There's a time and place for everything.' She shot Hugo a quick grin. 'Maybe it's a maturity thing. You're about the same age as Brian.'

Hugo was silent. He didn't like the comparison.

Maggie was still grinning. 'You didn't try and tone me down, I noticed.'

This time Hugo returned the grin. Maybe he wasn't drop-dead boring after all. Just safe, as Maggie had said. And safe sounded much nicer than boring. 'Would it have had any effect?'

Maggie's grin widened. 'Probably not.'

'There you go, then.' Hugo's expression sobered. 'And you obviously knew what you were doing. You're very skilled.' He pulled the Jeep to a halt but paused before opening his door. 'You did a fantastic job there, Maggie. I was really impressed.'

'Thanks.' Maggie followed Hugo into the house, trying to keep her pace measured. She felt more like skipping. Hugo had never been 'really impressed' with her that she could remember. He had sounded almost proud of her and the pleasure it was giving her was enough to make her toes tingle. She could feel her cheeks getting pinker as well and it wasn't due to the weather conditions.

'It's still cold, isn't it? Shall we crank up the fire and heat some soup?'

The lunch was leisurely and neither Hugo nor Maggie were in any hurry to leave the warmth of the fire when they finished eating. The weather was closing in again.

'Not really nice enough to go sightseeing, is it?'

'No.' Maggie made space for Lass to climb up on the

couch beside her. 'To be honest, your idea of browsing through journals seems like a nice way to spend the afternoon.'

'Help yourself.' Hugo waved at the pile on the coffee-table.

It was a surprisingly enjoyable few hours. Maggie found plenty of articles of interest and Hugo was quite happy to have his own reading interrupted to answer any queries she came up with. Periodically, they wondered aloud how the Barkers were getting on and by five o'clock, Hugo couldn't wait any longer. He put a call through to the coronary care unit in Dunedin and spoke at length to one of the consultants. He was smiling broadly by the time he finished the call.

'They tried to abort what was looking like a major inferior infarct with angioplasty but they ran into difficulty so he got taken straight to Theatre and they went ahead with bypass surgery. He's just out of Theatre and in Intensive Care, and so far everything's looking good.'

'That's fantastic!'

'Sure is. Calls for a celebration, I think. How about a glass of wine?'

'Double fantastic.'

Sharing a bottle of red in front of the fire was a noticeable improvement on an already very pleasant afternoon. The cold and now dark and wet evening was forgotten even by the dogs, who gave no indication that they might need to be let outside.

Hugo raised his second glass of wine. 'Here's to you, Maggie. For making the inspired decision to come and live in Central Otago.'

Maggie drank the toast happily and then held up her own glass. 'Here's to Charlie,' she said. 'May he make a full and speedy recovery.'

Hugo drank to that toast. 'Here's to your skill with speedy driving.' He grinned. 'A trip with you makes me appreciate being alive.'

But he didn't raise his glass any further to reach his lips. And neither did Maggie. For a long moment they stared at each other.

'It wasn't my fault, you know, Hugh,' Maggie said softly. 'The accident.'

'I know that.'

'It wasn't Fliss's fault either. That bus came round the corner completely on the wrong side of the road.'

'I know.'

'It hadn't even been my idea to go to Athens. Fliss was so set on seeing the Acropolis.'

Hugo tried to smile. 'I can believe that.'

'It felt like my fault, though,' Maggie whispered. 'And I know you blamed me.'

'I didn't,' Hugo said slowly. 'Not really.'

'You never answered my letters.'

'I had trouble coping for a while.' Hugo was turning his glass round and round in his hands, staring at the blood-red liquid it contained. 'I blamed myself as much as anyone else. I took responsibility for Fliss after Dad died. She could talk Mum into anything. It was always my role to be the sensible one. To point out the dangers. To try and look after her.'

'And I was always the one getting her into trouble, wasn't I?' Maggie's eyes shone with unshed tears.

'You were always the one she wanted to be with.' Hugo used the last of the wine in his glass to wash away the lump in his throat. 'And you always had such fun together.'

'Until something went wrong.' Maggie sniffed and rubbed her nose with the back of her hand. 'Do you remember that time we decided to be fairies and try flying around the living room? We broke that precious ornament of your mother's.'

'The china shepherdess?' Hugo's smile was lopsided as he reached for the bottle to refill his glass. 'You put all the pieces into a shoebox and hid them in my bedroom.'

'And you spent hours gluing it back together. It was months before she spotted the cracks.'

'And do you remember the time you decided you'd both look good with jet-black hair? You must have been about twelve or thirteen.'

Maggie chuckled softly. 'Fliss looked like a vampire and my hair turned that weird sort of bottle-green shade.'

'And what about the time you went to the movies and missed the last bus home and decided to try hitch-hiking?'

'You were *so* cross.'

'You were both lucky you found a ride with someone decent.'

'I knew he was safe enough. He had grey hair and a dog collar.'

'It was still a damned stupid thing to have done. You were only fifteen.'

'I knew you'd tell us off.'

'Didn't need to, did I?' Hugo was smiling now. 'Inviting him in for a cup of tea and an off-the-cuff sermon did the trick.'

'It was awful,' Maggie groaned. 'We thought he was never going to stop and I didn't dare look at Fliss, 'cause I would have started giggling and you would have been even more furious.' Maggie looked up at Hugo and suddenly the tears overflowed. 'Oh, Hugh. I still miss her *so* much.'

Hugo stood up and then Maggie was in his arms and he was holding her tightly.

'So do I,' he murmured.

'And I missed you, too,' Maggie snuffled. 'And I thought you blamed me and would never want to see me again.'

'I don't blame you,' Hugo said. And, finally, it was true. 'Fliss loved you. She had the happiest moments of her life with you. And maybe, thanks to you, she had more of them in just nineteen years than some people get after living for sixty years.' His mouth was against Maggie's hair. He could feel the softness of it with his lips as he spoke. 'I'll bet you had all sorts of adventures in Europe that I never heard about.'

'I've got lots of photos.' Maggie's words were muffled by Hugo's shoulder. 'Would you like to see them?'

'Sure.' Hugo nodded. 'But not just yet.'

Maggie pulled away to look up at Hugo. 'Will it ever stop hurting like this?' she whispered.

'I think it might,' Hugo said gently. 'Especially if we can remember the good things.'

'It seems a lifetime ago some days,' Maggie said. 'And then it seems like only yesterday.'

'It was a long time ago.' Hugo pushed a stray tendril of hair back from where it was caught on Maggie's damp eyelashes. 'You were both just kids.'

'I grew up fast.' Maggie managed a watery smile.

Hugo smiled back. She had grown up all right. Maggie might still need the kind of comfort he'd given her as a child, but he was holding a woman in his arms now. She might still have the spirit of the irrepressible child he remembered but she had a wisdom and strength and confidence that was new...and extraordinary.

And very disturbing. Hugo could actually feel his awareness of Maggie evolving. He could sense with a kind of detachment the reaction his body was having to her.

The recognition that she was an attractive woman had suddenly become rather personal. She was attractive to *him*, and the acknowledgment of her sexuality felt like a betrayal of all they had ever had between them.

Maggie saw the rapid changes in Hugo's expression and could feel a mirror image of the emotions they portrayed. A shared grief as well as joy. Forgiveness for any past misdemeanours or judgements. The recognition that they were both long past adolescence—and with that came that split second of shared desire that seemed so inappropriate in the wake of remembering the trust and love they had forged over so many years. The roles they had always kept firmly within were no longer there. Maggie didn't need a big brother. She wasn't an extension of Hugo's family any more.

Had it, in fact, been only she who had felt that sharp twinge of desire? That expression had been so fleeting in Hugo's eyes that she could easily imagine it had never happened. Maybe she had simply projected an awakening of her old feelings. Had Hugo recognised it enough to be embarrassed or even appalled? Something was certainly enough to make him almost push her away. To make a show of putting more wood on the fire and then snapping his fingers at the dogs.

'Come on, you lot. I don't care if it's snowing again. You need some fresh air.'

Hugo needed some fresh air as well and, for once, Maggie wasn't making any attempt to join them. The thought that she might have seen something of what he'd felt in his face was horrifying and he couldn't blame her for turning away in embarrassment. She'd held him in a position of trust all her life. Hugo hesitated by the front door. He couldn't break that trust now. Maggie needed to know she was still safe with him.

'Don't forget your hat if you're coming with us,' he called over his shoulder. 'It *is* snowing again out here.'

CHAPTER SIX

'IT'S cute.'

Maggie stared from the passenger seat window of the ambulance at a property enhanced by a sunny winter's afternoon. On the edge of the central business district in Queenstown, it was one of a line of what looked like doll's houses. The gardens, if there were any, would be adjacent to the back of a row of shops. The houses were old and square with tiny verandahs. The example Maggie was peering at had the winter skeleton of a rampant climbing rose obscuring some decorative ironwork gracing the verandah's curved iron roof.

'It's bigger than it looks.' Jason drove the heavy vehicle half onto the footpath of the narrow street so that they wouldn't obstruct traffic. 'There's four bedrooms.' He opened the driver's door and jumped out. 'Come and have a look. They're not expecting us at the medical centre for fifteen minutes yet.'

Maggie followed a little less enthusiastically. She hadn't said she was definitely interested in the upcoming vacancy in Jason's flat, just that it sounded like a possibility. Now she was here, she wasn't sure that it even ranked that highly.

'You're really close to the shops, aren't you?' Maggie was careful not to make it sound like a criticism and she obviously succeeded.

'Great, isn't it? We hardly ever cook. The restaurants and take-aways are brilliant. And we're within easy walking distance of all the pubs and clubs.' Jason grinned at

Maggie. 'We never have to worry about driving home if we've been out for a bit of a rave.'

'That's handy.' Maggie wondered how often Jason and his friends hit the club scene. Not that it mattered. She'd been working with Jason for over a month now and she had no complaints. He was a competent ambulance officer who loved his job and was keen to advance his training. He was good company and reliable. He was also young at only twenty-five, good-looking and popular, and Maggie would be the last person to suggest that someone should tone down and get less enjoyment out of his life. She stepped over a dodgy-looking broken board on the verandah and waited while Jason unlocked the front door. 'Doesn't it get a bit noisy some nights?' she ventured.

'Yeah.' Jason's dreadlocks bounced as he nodded. 'Queenstown really rocks. You'll love it.'

Maggie said nothing. The thought that the silence and peace of Hugo's lakeside haven was preferable wasn't something she could share with Jason unless she didn't mind sounding like someone's grandmother.

'You go ahead.' Jason waved her on. 'The kitchen's down the end.'

Maggie walked down a narrow, dark central hallway into a kitchen-living area at the back of the house. A man of about Jason's age stood by the bench wearing nothing but a pair of board shorts. Tall, blond and lean, he had bright blue eyes and a friendly smile. Very friendly.

'So what do you think?' Jason was saying behind her. 'Nice?'

Maggie couldn't help returning the smile the Greek god was bestowing upon her. 'Very nice,' she murmured.

'Oh…' Jason had spotted the god now. 'Hi, Sven. You're up already!' He turned to Maggie. 'Sven's a ski instructor,' he told her.

'No kidding?' Maggie tried to rein in her smile so that she didn't come across as being totally inane, but so far Sven was by far the most attractive feature of the flat.

'Maggie's thinking of taking over Donna's room,' Jason told Sven. 'Cool, eh?'

'Very cool.' Sven's accent was another bonus. 'Do you ski, Maggie?'

'Not yet,' Maggie said happily. 'But I'm thinking of taking lessons.' Heavens, now she sounded like a wannabe ski bunny.

'How's the day off going?' Jason asked his flatmate. 'We don't usually see you out of bed before lunchtime.'

'Lisa had to work,' Sven said sadly. 'No point staying in bed.'

Jason laughed. 'Lisa is Sven's roommate,' he informed Maggie. 'That's how we get five of us living here and keep the rent down so well.'

'Oh.' Maggie let her gaze roam as Sven's attraction faded into insignificance. The living room was tiny. Did everyone spend their time in their own rooms or were they all too busy with the club scene to worry about lack of space at home? There weren't too many worries felt about cleaning up either. Ski boots lay on piles of newspaper and magazines. Dirty dishes lay in corners and empty beer cans littered the hearth.

'It's my turn to clean up this week.' Jason grimaced as he noticed the direction of Maggie's gaze. 'I'll get round to it soon.'

'I'm not the tidiest person on earth myself,' Maggie confessed.

'Come on, I'll show you the rest of the house.' Jason turned his back on the mess. 'This is Erin's room. You met her the night we all went out to dinner, remember?'

Maggie nodded. 'How's her arm?'

'She's due to get her cast off next week so she should be back to full duties at the hospital again.'

'That's great. They're still very short-staffed.' It would be nice having another cheerful face around her working environment. As a flatmate Maggie could imagine that Erin would be just as good company as Jason was.

'This is Donna's room, right beside the bathroom.' Jason's grin was cheeky. 'That'll be useful for a lady of your advancing years.'

'Cheers, mate.' Maggie poked her head around the door.

The room had just enough space for a single bed. A row of skis stood propped along the wall and a backpack took up the space beneath a window that looked out on the dustbins at the back of a restaurant. Maggie thought of her bedroom at Hugo's house with the French doors opening to the verandah and the endless view of the lake and mountains. She couldn't repress a small sigh. She really didn't want to move at all. Disguising the motive for the sigh by simultaneously checking her watch, she turned away from the room.

'Time we went back to work, I think. What was the name of our patient again?'

'Dulcie Payne. I've been out to her more than once.' Jason climbed back into the driver's seat of the ambulance. 'She's in her eighties and has bad Alzheimer's but her husband refuses to have her put in a rest home. She wanders off at regular intervals so we get called out to help look for her sometimes.' He started the engine and eased the ambulance along the narrow street. 'Last time she didn't recognise Tom and refused to go home with him. Whacked him in the face and he got a nosebleed that wouldn't stop.'

'Poor man,' Maggie murmured. 'She's being admitted

to hospital now. Is that an interim step before rest-home placement?'

'Doubt it. Tom's determined to look after her. They tried admitting her for assessment last time but he refused. Said she looked after him for their whole marriage and he's going to look after her now or die trying.'

'He sounds like a nice man,' Maggie said. 'What a sad position to be in at this stage of their lives.'

'Yeah.' Jason indicated that he was turning into the medical centre. 'I'm not going to get old.'

'Oh, sure.' Maggie grinned at her partner. 'Let me know the secret when you find it.'

'Too late.' Jason shook his head sadly. 'I know a lost cause when I see one.'

Maggie was still glaring at Jason when the door to the medical centre opened. She shouldn't have been surprised by Hugo's appearance, seeing as it was his day to work at the centre. So why did her pulse rate leap quite that much? And why was she so conscious of the length of time that passed whenever they made eye contact with each other?

She knew why, of course. She tried to listen to what Hugo was saying with professional interest.

'This might not be easy,' he warned the crew. 'Tom doesn't want Dulcie in hospital even for respite care, but his chronic respiratory problems have been exacerbated by a chest infection so there's no way he can manage at home for the next few days.'

'Does he want to come to the hospital with her?'

'That would be great. I can take him home again later.' Hugo's gaze caught Maggie's again. 'It won't help Tom's breathing if he gets upset by all this.'

'I'll take good care of them both,' Maggie promised. 'And Jason's really good with old people.'

'Sure am,' Jason agreed. He winked at Maggie. 'I get a lot of experience with them on this job.'

The satisfactory management of a potentially difficult patient transfer and even Jason's continued humorous jabs at Maggie's seniority failed to lift the uncharacteristically sombre mood for Maggie that had been provoked by the tour of Jason's flat. She tried to snap out of it as she used a quiet spell to catch up on paperwork. It wasn't as though there was any real urgency to find new accommodation, was there?

The new tension she was feeling in being close to Hugo was only *her* problem. The conversation they'd had about Felicity over a week ago had marked a change in their relationship. A change for the better in that it enabled the kind of closeness they'd had in the past to re-emerge. It had been fostered by sharing memories and photo albums and it removed any awkwardness in sharing living quarters as adults. They knew so much about each other and had done for so long that the acceptance of any faults in the other was as automatic as within any family. But that was the problem as well.

They weren't family and never had been. And while Hugo could not be haunted by any memories of a teenage crush, the desire that had been rekindled for Maggie was becoming harder to ignore with every passing day. The awareness was there every time she saw him. The knot that was half excitement and half something much deeper caught her stomach with increasing intensity. Maggie knew she watched him too often, allowing her gaze to rest on his face when she thought he wasn't looking. Or, worse, watching the way his jeans moulded themselves to his thighs as he strode ahead of her on the beach as they walked the dogs. Or simply enjoying the sight of his hands as they held a journal he was reading by the fire in the evening. Maggie would look at the strong hands with their fine cover of dark hair, the long and skilful-looking fingers, and she could turn that knot in her abdomen into the most delicious tingles by imagining what it would feel like to have those hands on her body.

Hugo couldn't possibly be aware of how she felt because it wasn't as though there was the slightest chance of it being reciprocated. Hugo hadn't moved past his assumed role as a pseudo-brother. And even if he had, he had Joan in his life and Maggie wasn't into stealing men. No. This was *her* problem all right and she either had to deal with it or move out. The only potential place she had to move into right now was Jason's flat. Living with a colleague wasn't a long-term solution and Maggie wasn't desperate for a quick fix. Yet. There had to be another way of distracting herself. That way she could find out whether she was merely revisiting that teenage crush or whether she had a major emotional disaster looming.

The checklist on her desk of equipment due for servicing caught Maggie's eye. She made a note to add the battery charger for the life pack to the list. Jason had alerted her to the fact that the charger was malfunctioning intermittently. The regulators for the oxygen cylinders were outdated as well and Maggie didn't trust them. She made another note to investigate the cost of replacement and to check the station's budget situation. Then she started doodling on the edge of the paper. If they wanted new regulators they would probably have to do some fundraising, as the hospital was doing to obtain updated resuscitation equipment, including a new ventilator, for the emergency department.

The distraction was immediate and Maggie swung in her chair to stare at the calendar on her wall. The fundraising ball was only two weeks away now and she had done nothing about obtaining a ticket or thinking about a costume. Having had her own idea of a fancy-dress ball embraced so whole-heartedly by the local community committee in charge of the fundraising venture, it would not reflect very well on the ambulance service if she failed to participate with due enthusiasm. Was it Hugo's reticence that had made the event less appealing? Maggie had asked him only a few days ago what he was planning to dress up as.

'I have no idea,' he'd said grumpily. 'Joan's organising that for me. She's going to hire something for both of us on one of her trips to Dunedin.'

'Don't you have a preference?'

'I'd prefer not to be going. I hate fancy dress. Whose idea was it, anyway?'

'Mine,' Maggie reminded him stiffly. 'But don't worry. I'm sure Joan will think of an appropriate costume for you.' Hugo's lack of interest felt like a reprimand. 'Dracula might be good,' she suggested blandly. 'I can just see you with those teeth and a bit of blood dripping down your chin.' She ignored Hugo's increasingly mutinous expression. 'The cloak would look good when you dance, too.'

'I hate dancing.'

Maggie's jaw had dropped. How could anybody hate dancing? Maybe Hugo *was* a bit stuffy after all. 'Dracula would be perfect, then,' she had said a little waspishly. 'We could borrow a coffin and you could lie there while everyone else is having fun.'

'What are you going as?' Hugo's retort had been swift. 'Pippi Longstocking?'

Maggie had spent quite a bit of time wondering if Hugo's suggestion had been an unkind reference to her unmanageable hair. It probably *would* poke out at right angles to her head if she tried braiding it. The reference could well have been a dig at her personality, however, and that was more hurtful. Did he really remember her behaviour as being outrageous? Did he still believe that Felicity had been lured into trouble by someone who had no respect for convention or constraint?

Maggie sighed heavily. The tension was there all right and it would continue growing unless she found a way of defusing it. She owed it to Hugo to find a solution. It wasn't his fault she felt the way she did. He'd hardly encouraged it, had he? He had, in fact, been kind enough to offer her a place to live and a chance to find peace with the terrible event that had separated them all those years ago. She had known before she'd come that he was in a relationship and it had never occurred to her that it would matter. She'd never had a chance with Hugo Patterson.

And she never would.

The ringing of the phone served to punctuate the dead end of that train of thought. That the call would present a possible solution to the impasse occurred to Maggie quite swiftly. And Donald Hamilton seemed only too happy to co-operate.

'A ball? Sounds fun, Maggie, I'd love to come. It would be good to see you. That's really why I was ringing.'

'Oh?' Maggie tried to sound cautiously pleased.

'I felt like planning a weekend away and I thought I'd take a chance and see whether you might be free for dinner or a day's skiing or something.'

'I'll get you a ticket, then. It's on Saturday the sixteenth. One of the biggest hotels is putting it on in their conference facility so it should be a good evening.'

'Is there a theme or do we just choose any kind of costume?'

'It's "Come as your favourite book character or movie star" so it's pretty wide-ranging.'

'What are you going as? Do you want me to hire a costume in town for you?'

'I'm sure I can dig something up.' Maggie twirled her chair around. Donald had a very nice voice. Deep. And warm. Quite sensual, really. 'I did some belly-dancing classes years ago. I could get my mother to post down my costume and go as something from *Aladdin*.'

'Mmm.' Donald's tone was approving. 'I'll have to think up something to match. Tell you what, let's have lunch if you're not out on the road when I'm down for my clinic next week. We can throw a few ideas around.'

It was astonishing how much effort had been put into the event. Hugo was quite blown away by the opulence of the venue and the support the community appeared to be giving to the fundraiser. The hospital was clearly a popular beneficiary and the contribution made by local and even international business interests was impressive. The decorations, lighting and bar facilities were lavish and the crowd unexpectedly large. Hugo was surprised to see that a number of the hospital's visiting specialists had made the effort to be present along with an almost full contingent of the local GPs and their partners, hospital staff and representatives from all the emergency services.

The sleek dinner suit Joan had chosen for him to wear had seemed like an inspired choice. He could tell everyone he was dressed as James Bond and could neatly avoid the loss of dignity he associated with dressing up in silly costumes. It also solved the problem of being on call. He wouldn't have to try changing in a hurry or, worse, turn up at the hospital dressed as someone like Dracula if he had an emergency call. Now that he was here, however, Hugo felt out of place. He looked more like one of the live band members or waiters than an active party participant. It was a boring costume. Even Joan's choice had been adventurous in comparison.

'I'm Julie Andrews,' she had explained in response to his astonishment on arriving to collect her. 'You know, *The Sound Of Music*?'

'It suits you.' Hugo had managed a smile. 'Just don't make a habit of it, will you?'

So, here he was. In a suit. With a nun standing beside him. An oasis of boring black and white in a sea of colour and imagination. Various animals, devils and gypsies were all around. He spotted one of the more conservative GPs dressed as Frankenstein and that quiet nurse, Megan, was a rather naughty-looking French maid. Even Lizzie had made a superlative effort and was looking magnificent in a medieval gown and elaborate headdress. Hugo's gaze kept roving. He was looking for Maggie, who had refused to tell him what she was planning to wear, which had only increased his curiosity. Or was it trepidation? He still had no idea because she had vanished from home early in her normal jeans and bright sweater. She was going to a pre-ball party with Jason and some other ambulance officers who were planning to get ready, *en masse*, at Jason's flat.

'Dr Patterson, did you forget it was fancy dress?' The young receptionist, Anne, was a clown with a lime-green wig and a brightly painted face.

'No. I'm James Bond.'

'Oh…right.' An enthusiastic-looking cowboy was pulling Anne towards the dance floor. 'Have fun!'

'This is great, isn't it, Hugh?' The chairman of the hospital's board of trustees raised his glass beside Hugo. 'Best fundraiser we've ever had. We might even manage to get that ultrasound equipment as well as the ventilator out of the profits.'

'It's wonderful,' Hugo agreed. 'I had no idea we'd get

a response like this.' The extravagant 'Henry the Eighth'
costume of his companion made the dinner suit seem even
more ordinary, if that were possible.

'Everyone's dancing, Hugh.' Joan was still standing loy-
ally by his side on the edge of the huge room.

'So they are.' Hugo could see another black robed figure
nearby. 'Look, you've got a partner. There's a priest over
there.'

'It's Lewis.' Joan's wave at the respiratory physician
was not acknowledged. 'We happened to meet up in the
costume hire shop. I think he's trying to be Sean Connery.'

'He should have chosen a monk's robe, then, not a
priest's.'

Joan shrugged. 'Whatever. Let's dance, Hugh.'

'Mmm.' Hugo had just caught sight of a new surge of
people entering. An excited group of young people that
rippled with laughter and exuded the intention of having
a good time. Jason made an eye-catching Superman with
his blond dreadlocks. Erin Willoughby was Cat Woman
and Maggie was…

Maggie was stunning, that's what she was. She had bare
feet with brightly painted red toenails and ankle bracelets
beneath softly billowing harem pants. A bra top dripping
with sequins did nothing to detract from the sparkling
'jewel' where her belly button should have been. Her hair
was unrestrained by any fastening of side locks and it
framed heavily made-up eyes that were all the more alluring thanks to the tiny veil obscuring her mouth. And who
was the Arab holding the hand that emerged from the arm-
load of coloured bangles? Hugo couldn't be sure at this
distance but he was fairly certain it was Donald Hamilton.
He looked away. He didn't want Maggie to spot him. Not
looking so much like a spectator. He cleared his throat.

'Come on, then.' He turned back to Joan and held out his hand. 'Let's dance.'

The music was great and the floor popular enough for any lack of style on Hugo's part to go unnoticed. It was also hot and Joan soon discovered that habits were not designed to make vigorous activity comfortable. Hugo was quite happy to follow her to the quieter area surrounding the bar. There were a lot of older members of the community watching the dancing and Hugo knew he should make a point of speaking to as many of the hospital's supporters as he could. Many of them were in evening dress, as he was, but somehow it didn't make Hugo happy to find he now fitted in.

'Joan—there you are! I've been looking for you.' Lewis Evans, the priest, emerged from the dance floor. 'I've got some news.'

Hugo had to turn at the touch on his arm. 'Dr Patterson? I'm Margo Smythe. My husband is the chairman of the local businessmen's association. He's very keen to make your acquaintance if you've got a free moment.'

Joan was moving away. 'It's about your painting,' Hugo heard Lewis telling her. 'The big one of Lake Hayes?'

Margo was pulling gently but firmly on Hugo's arm. 'We're wondering if you could tell us about this emergency equipment we're raising funds for. Jeremy's right over here. Can we buy you a drink?'

'Just juice, thanks,' Hugo said. 'I'm on call.'

Jeremy Smythe was several inches shorter than Hugo's six feet two inches. His shoulder presented no barrier to seeing what was happening on the dance floor and everyone appeared to be having great fun. Especially Maggie. She danced with the kind of joyous abandon with which she approached most things in life. Right now she seemed to be giving a growing number of devotees a lesson in belly-dancing.

Later, when Hugo spotted her in the supper room, her face veil had vanished and she was still the centre of a group which was clearly having much more fun than he was. It *was* Donald Hamilton with Maggie and, judging by his constant grinning, he was enjoying himself immensely. Hugo's mood dived another notch or two. Being merely a spectator made him feel like a boulder in a swiftly flowing river. A big, black boulder. Maybe it was better that he stood on the sidelines so he didn't disrupt the flow. Even Joan was enjoying herself…somewhere. It took Hugo some time to find her when a call from the hospital gave him the excuse to extricate himself from the fundraising committee's company.

'I've got to go,' he told her. 'Sounds like someone's come in with a CVA.'

'Oh, no!' Joan had discarded her head covering and the white bib. The robe was now exposing a hint of cleavage that Hugo hadn't known she possessed. 'And this is such fun!' She was smiling happily. 'Do you know what Lewis told me?' She didn't wait for a response from Hugo. 'One of my paintings has sold! The gallery wants more. Maybe even a whole exhibition.'

'That's fantastic. Congratulations!'

It's exciting, isn't it? Lewis bought me a bottle of champagne to celebrate. Would you like some?'

'I'm on call,' Hugo reminded her. 'On my way to see a patient right now, in fact. I came to find you so I could give you a ride home.'

'Oh…' Joan looked past Hugo and then smiled again. 'Don't worry about me. I'm sure Lewis can take me home.'

'Of course I can.' Lewis tipped the bottle he held over Joan's empty glass. 'That is, if it's OK with Hugh.'

'It's fine. Thanks, Lewis.'

'Maybe you should take Maggie home instead,' Joan suggested.

Hugo blinked in surprise. 'Why do you say that?'

'Well…' Joan's lips pressed together firmly as she shook her head. 'Lewis tells me that Donald's not divorced at all. His wife threw him out last year for a while but they've been back together since Christmas.'

'That's right,' Lewis confirmed. 'I had dinner with them only last week. His wife is quite convinced he's reformed.'

'You should do something about it,' Joan urged. 'Before their affair goes any further.'

'You don't *know* that they're having an affair,' Hugo said quietly. 'And even if they are, it's not really any of our business, is it?'

It was a relief to escape, to drive the few kilometres along deserted roads and then spend time at the hospital being distracted by someone else's worries. The middle-aged woman who'd been brought in by ambulance was reassured to learn that her neurological symptoms had most likely been caused by a migraine rather than anything more sinister. She was even happier to stay in the hospital for overnight observation. Hugo used the opportunity to catch up on a couple of other inpatients, including Nancy, who still hadn't come quite right after her bout of pneumonia. Her heart failure was a lot harder to control now and she was getting very little rest because she became very short of breath lying down. He wasn't surprised to find her sitting bolt upright and wide awake when he stopped by her bed.

'Goodness me, Hugo. What are you doing here at this time of night?'

'I had to come in for an emergency. I thought I'd just pop up and see how you were, Nancy.' Hugo spoke very quietly so as not to disturb the sleeping patients around them.

'I'm about the same, dear,' Nancy told him. 'I don't really expect to get much better this time, you know.' Clouded blue eyes gazed at Hugo in the dim light. 'You're very dressed up.'

'I've been to a party,' Hugo told her. He had his hand on Nancy's wrist now, hoping to find her heart rhythm more regular than it had been. It wasn't and he sighed.

'It can't have been a very good party,' Nancy observed.

Hugo smiled. Nancy could see things a lot of people couldn't. She was very old. And probably very wise. 'I felt a bit left out, actually,' he surprised himself by admitting. 'Everyone else was in fancy dress.'

'Why not you?'

'I'm not sure,' Hugo confessed. 'I've always thought fancy dress was silly. Embarrassing. Tonight I wondered if being sensible was just making me miss out on something.'

Nancy patted his hand. 'It would only do that if you were being sensible for the sake of others and not yourself.'

Hugo pondered this for a moment. Maybe he'd been sensible for the sake of others for so long that it had just become a part of him.

'Being sensible isn't a bad thing,' Nancy said softly. Then she smiled. 'Being silly occasionally doesn't hurt either. Life's shorter than you think, dear. You've got to make the most of it.'

Hugo switched off an echo of similar sentiments he'd heard Maggie express as he returned the smile. This was certainly an occasion that called for a sensible approach.

'It's time you got some rest, Nancy. I'm going to get the nurses to put you on oxygen again and we'll see if that helps a bit.'

It was only sensible that Hugo got some rest too. He arrived home shortly after two a.m. but any thought of heading straight to bed dissipated as he noticed how empty the house felt. Maggie wasn't home yet. Maybe she wasn't coming home. Perhaps she was, at this very moment, tucked up in some hotel suite with the very unsuitable Donald Hamilton. The cardiologist's personal life might very well be none of Hugo's business but he couldn't apply the same lack of involvement to Maggie. He *cared* about what happened to her, damn it!

Maggie was shivering as she let herself into the house. Harem trousers and a bra top were vastly unsuitable attire for the depths of a Central Otago winter. Nice of Hugo to leave the fire going and a light on, Maggie thought gratefully. It was very welcoming.

Far more welcoming than the expression on Hugo's face. She was startled to find him standing in front of the fire, his feet planted far enough apart to make him look almost intimidating.

'It's three a.m.!' he informed her. 'Where the hell have you been, Maggie?'

'You know perfectly well where I've been,' Maggie retorted. 'You were there yourself.' She rubbed at her bare arms but didn't want to move closer to the fire just yet. She stared at Hugo. 'You weren't waiting up for me, were you?'

'As a matter of fact, I was.'

'What on earth for?'

Hugo was taken aback by the astonishment in Maggie's voice. The anger that had sneaked up on him over the last hour now seemed inappropriate but he couldn't just shake it off. Especially not with Maggie standing there half-naked and looking so damned…attractive.

'There's something you should know, Maggie.'

'And what's that?'

'Donald Hamilton is not divorced.'

'No,' Maggie agreed. 'He's separated.'

'So why is he still living with his wife?'

'*Is* he?'

Hugo ignored the warning note. 'And his kids,' he added for good measure. 'Lewis Evans had dinner with them last week.'

Maggie's chin lifted defiantly. Donald had been perfectly pleasant company for the evening. She had had fun. Enough fun to distract her from wanting to be with Hugo, in fact. Donald hadn't even got pushy when she'd declined his invitation to visit his room for a nightcap. His intention to get her into his bed had been transparent and Maggie wasn't ready to test the distraction level that far but maybe it would have been preferable to standing here feeling like a teenager who had broken curfew and was now about to be given a lecture on morals.

'This is none of your business, Hugh.'

'Yes, it is. I care about you.'

'I care about *you*,' Maggie shot back. 'But I wouldn't dream of telling you how unsuitable Joan is.'

'That's because she's *not* unsuitable.'

'That's a matter of opinion.'

Hugo was not going to be sidetracked. 'At least she's not married to someone else.'

'Maybe Donald isn't either, despite what you've heard. And even if he is, it's *my* business to find out.' Maggie let her breath out in an angry huff. 'For heaven's sake, Hugh. I don't need protection. I'm *not* your little sister.'

The moment's silence was heavy. Maggie knew it had been a sharp dig but she'd had enough.

'And, in case you haven't noticed, Hugh, I'm not a child any more.' Maggie's feet seemed to move without conscious effort. Suddenly she was standing right in front of Hugo. 'I'm all grown up, Hugh,' she said softly. 'I can do what I want, *when* I want to. Just like you.'

Maggie's feet were still moving. She stretched right up on tiptoe and planted a brief kiss directly on Hugo's lips. Then she simply turned and walked from the room, pausing at the door to speak into the stunned silence she was leaving behind her.

'Goodnight, Hugh,' she said calmly. 'Sleep well.'

CHAPTER SEVEN

SLEEPING well was completely out of the question.

Sleeping at all would have been a bonus. Hugo had never felt quite this disturbed in his life. The kiss had been nothing. A brief touch of lips prompted by Maggie's determination to prove she was an independent adult. A split second of physical contact that hadn't even been particularly intimate, and yet it had had the effect of an explosion somewhere deep in the foundations upon which Hugo had built his life.

He couldn't put his finger on precisely where the damage had occurred. He just knew, beyond any doubt, that something important was now very, very unstable. Analysis that would lead to identification and then repair was vital. However much his body tried to persuade him otherwise, the restful oblivion of sleep was a luxury Hugo couldn't afford to indulge in right now.

Maggie probably had no idea that she had vaulted over an unspoken boundary. She had kissed and hugged him countless times in her life after all. It wasn't as though a chaste kiss on the lips was any more significant than a peck on the cheek. So why did it *feel* so damned significant? And why, in heaven's name, did it never feel remotely like that when he kissed Joan? Or any of the other women he'd kissed in his life for that matter? Hugo groaned, a sound of faint despair that was easily muffled by his pillow as he turned yet again in search of comfort.

He wanted her. There was no denying it now. Maybe the first cracks had appeared when he had recognised what an attractive woman she had become and that he was affected by that attraction. Admitting an attraction was one thing, however. Perfectly understandable. Controllable. The shock of experiencing what could only be considered frank lust was something quite different. And quite unacceptable. And what the hell was he going to do about it? He was living with her. He saw her first thing in the morning with those gold-flecked eyes still clouded by dreams and hair that had yet to be tamed by product. He saw her last thing at night, curled up and looking as much a part of his home as the dogs that crowded her so lovingly now.

What if he admitted how he felt and suggested it would be better if she moved out? No. Hugo turned again and stared into the darkness towards his ceiling. To admit the desire would be to destroy the level of trust and friendship he had with Maggie. She would be shocked. And she would lose what Hugo had always tried to be for her. A brother. A father figure almost. To resign that position could be enough to send Maggie straight into the arms of the older man already in the wings.

The thought of Donald Hamilton was enough to cause an unpleasant clenching in Hugo's gut. Had she kissed *him*? Was this new and unpleasant sensation *jealousy*? Hugo forced himself to take a deep breath and relax. No. It was just a deep unease. A conviction that Maggie was heading for trouble just as she had done so often in the past. And if Hugo sent her away he would be able to do nothing to protect her. Nothing to help glue the pieces back together after disaster had occurred.

He couldn't ask her to leave and there was no real reason to. This was his problem, not Maggie's, and he could deal with it. Lust was a transient phenomenon, especially when it carried this amount of heat. It would burn itself out and disappear. If he kept it well enough hidden it would not cause any damage to a relationship that Hugo had no intention of harming.

'How did you sleep?' Maggie was looking disgustingly refreshed when Hugo entered the kitchen the next morning.

'Fine, thanks,' Hugo lied. He blinked gritty eyes as he looked at the pot Maggie was stirring enthusiastically. 'What on earth are you cooking?'

'Porridge. I thought it might be just what the doctor would order for a chilly winter morning.'

Hugo grunted noncommittally as he stepped a little closer and peered at the bubbling contents of the pot. 'Porridge is a bit boring, isn't it?'

'Not when you have brown sugar and whipped cream on it.' Maggie licked her lips and Hugo turned away abruptly.

It was bad enough that Maggie was only half-dressed in an ancient T-shirt and track pants. The gap between the shirt and pants might be barely noticeable but in conjunction with her bare feet and bright toenails it was far too reminiscent of her belly-dancer's costume. And the sight of a small, pink tongue wetting expectant lips was way too much to handle after last night's contemplations. Maybe controlling how he felt was going to be far more traumatic than he had anticipated. How long would it take for lust to burn itself out anyway? Days? Weeks? *Months?* Hugo slumped into a chair at the end of the table with a sigh he had no hope of suppressing.

'You sound tired.' Maggie placed a bowl of porridge in front of Hugo and sat down to one side of him.

'I'm fine,' Hugo growled. There were six chairs at this table. Why did Maggie have to sit within touching distance?

'Have some cream.' Maggie's finger collected a blob of

whipped cream as she passed him the bowl. She popped her finger in her mouth and sucked it clean with obvious relish. 'Mmm,' she smiled. 'Yum.'

Hugo closed his eyes in a very deliberate blink. Distraction was needed here. And it was urgent. Opening his eyes, he caught sight of the journal abandoned, probably by Maggie, in the centre of the dining table. Fortunately Maggie didn't notice his haste in grabbing the potential rescue material. She was too busy spooning sugar onto her hot porridge and watching it melt into sticky, brown puddles.

'I really must catch up on some reading.' Hugo tried to sound casual. 'And it's about time I wrote up some of the interesting case histories I've collected. I might go through my files today when I've finished my ward round.'

'Really?' Maggie's expression suggested that it was not an ideal way to spend a Sunday. It probably ranked quite highly on a rating scale for inducing boredom, in fact, but as Hugo watched a spoonful of porridge enter her mouth before he could drag his eyes away he knew it was his only possible salvation.

If he spent more time at the hospital then he'd be spending less time in Maggie's company. Hugo finished his breakfast quickly and excused himself. A day away from home was definitely called for. In fact, more than a day might be just the solution he was searching for. The idea gained merit as Hugo drove towards the hospital. He could check out any upcoming conferences that appealed. It wouldn't be any problem arranging locum cover by the team of GPs in the area and he had accumulated conference and study leave for some time now. It always seemed such an effort to pull himself away from his routine, and that was ridiculous. He was far too young to be stuck in a rut and even if he didn't enjoy travelling particularly he would appreciate home even more when he returned.

He could go somewhere interesting. Adventurous, even. Acapulco or Egypt. That would impress Maggie. Might even show her that he had more than a little adventure in his soul. Hugo could just imagine showing her the photos and answering her eager questions. She'd probably say, more than once, 'I wish I'd been there,' and Hugo knew in that moment that the plan was a non-starter because *he'd* wish she had been there, too. The pleasure from the thought of sharing photos was insignificant compared with the notion of actually sharing the trip.

So what *was* the answer? Hugo marched along the main corridor of Lakeview Hospital with a heavy tread. He was several steps past a familiar picture hanging on the wall before a new notion presented itself. Could *Joan* be the answer? If nothing else, spending more time with Joan or even going away with her would be a guaranteed way of letting Maggie know she was safe. Then, even if he inadvertently let signs of his attraction to her slip, she would realise they meant nothing. But that would be using Joan and would a totally unacceptable form of behaviour.

Unless…

Hugo's path towards the medical ward continued automatically as his mind focussed on something entirely unprofessional. Unless he could divert what he felt for Maggie to someone far more suitable. Like Joan. Maybe that was more than half the problem, in fact. He was suffering the effects of a less than satisfactory love life. Hugo had to stifle something like a smile. Being a born-again virgin was not necessarily healthy. If he spent more time with Joan it was quite possible he could fall in lust. She was, after all, an attractive woman and a physical relationship might be just what was needed to tip the balance.

Hugo was quite confident that Joan would be receptive. All he needed was an opportunity or two to start turning up the heat.

By the time Hugo had completed a check on all his patients and spent some time in his office ignoring his filing cabinet he knew just how he could go about turning up that heat. He'd break the routine he and Joan had established. He could take her out to lunch instead of sharing a sandwich in the hospital staffroom with their colleagues. He could take her out for dinner on a Wednesday as well as Fridays. No, not Wednesday. That was Joan's painting-class evening. A night out at a club or just a quick drink after work might do it. That would be ideal. He could just drop the suggestion in towards the end of a day. It didn't have to be blatant. Even a casual invitation would be un-usual enough to surprise Joan. She would know instantly that something had changed. That a signal was being given.

Confident that a feasible resolution was now in progress, Hugo found he could divert enough of his attention to find real distraction in his work. It wasn't until he had spent a profitable afternoon engrossed in reading some fascinating medical literature and was driving home again that a re-finement to his plan came as added inspiration. The signal idea was great, but what would make it perfect would be to be able to do it in front of Maggie.

That way, the signal would work in two directions. Joan would know that, at last, he was serious about taking their friendship to a new level and Maggie would know that he was no threat. He was not going to use the position in her life to take advantage of her and he was certainly not going to risk losing the gift of what she had brought back into his life.

And it was a gift. Hugo only had to glimpse Maggie

running full tilt along the beach with the dogs in hot pursuit as he turned the Jeep into the woolshed to recognise that truth. Maggie was a link to his past. One that didn't need to be shut away any more. They could talk about Felicity now and her name was often dropped into a conversation without thought. It was only natural that they both wanted to remember someone they had both loved and now they could do it without the pain. Instead of keeping them apart, Felicity now provided a bond of enormous strength. A bond that Hugo could not possibly have with anyone else.

Quite apart from that bond, Maggie represented the kind of attitude to life that Hugo had always denied himself. A willingness to take risks. A headlong enthusiasm for living that was a joy to be near. In measured doses it was precisely what Hugo needed in his life. Maggie was a perfect friend and their past association allowed Hugo to embrace the extra dimension it provided for his own life without any threat to the larger picture he had framed for his future.

Hugo hesitated for just a moment before climbing out of his vehicle. He needed just one more reminder that Maggie couldn't possibly be anything more than a bonus before he could prepare himself to respond to the cheerful greeting he knew he was about to receive. Maggie was a wild card that added zest to a game. Added spice, like a few drops of her favourite chilli sauce to the glass of tomato juice that was Hugo's life. The awful metaphor made Hugo smile. Or did the wry amusement stem from the tiny seed of a notion that he and Maggie *could* be more than friends?

An entertaining notion, yes, but totally impractical. Hugo only had to compare Maggie to Joan to reinforce how ludicrous such a notion was, and that was precisely what he found himself doing over the next few days.

*   *   *

Monday was a busy day for both the hospital and the ambulance service. Far too busy to provide any opportunity for Hugo to follow through on his plan to break routine and surprise Joan with an unexpected invitation. Two deliveries, one requiring assistance with forceps, kept both Joan and the other midwife, Sue, under pressure. Maggie dealt with a diabetic in a hypoglycaemic crisis, an epileptic with uncontrollable seizures, two episodes of chest pain and an elderly woman with a fractured neck of femur. More than once, Hugo glanced out from a window of the hospital to see Maggie at the wheel of an ambulance, beacons already flashing as she headed out, the siren kicking in when the vehicle was just far enough away from the hospital not to disturb its inpatients. Maggie was off, full tilt, to deal with another emergency.

And Joan was coping with the potential difficulty of the young mother in labour with her usual efficiency. Awareness of the implications seemed to reinforce her calm approach and she was only too happy to call on Hugo's expertise and abdicate her position of being in control if necessary. Even as Hugo applied the forceps and helped the infant into the world, he was aware of a brief thought about Maggie. She was out there, somewhere, faced with heaven only knew what kind of problems and she would be coping, somehow, with whatever resources she could summon.

Joan's pleasure in the successful outcome of her case was perfectly sincere and professional, with just a hint of her own joy in handling a new baby. Maggie, on the other hand, was positively crowing with pleasure at the transformation IV glucose had produced in her combative and difficult diabetic patient. Joan still looked as clean and tidy as she had when she'd come on duty. Maggie's shirt-tail was hanging below the polar fleece vest she wore and her boots were scuffed and muddy.

Hugo almost tripped over those boots on Tuesday morning as he went to let the dogs out. The vest was lying over the arm of the couch and Maggie's stethoscope had been abandoned on the kitchen bench. Items of underwear drooped from the heated towel rails in the bathroom and Hugo was quite convinced now that the bottles and pots of feminine necessities on the window-sill were breeding. Joan's bathroom never looked like this. Not that that smooth blonde hair would ever need control from any kind of professional product, but if it did, Hugo could be absolutely certain that the container would be well hidden away. Hugo was smiling, however, as he dipped a finger into the little orange pot. He liked this fudge stuff. He never had to push his hair out of his eyes these days and it saved the hassle of having to fit such frequent haircuts into his schedule. His introduction to product was another little bonus of having Maggie around.

Joan wasn't at work on Tuesday and Hugo didn't have the time to make contact, being so busy fitting in the follow-ups on all the new inpatients Maggie had provided the previous day on top of his day at the medical centre. Joan had apparently kept herself busy at home because she had a new picture to show Hugo on Wednesday. A watercolour of autumn trees in Arrowtown.

'It's superb,' Hugo told her. 'You'll have to put it in the exhibition.'

It *was* a lovely picture. Muted but very attractive. A bit like Joan's character, really. Hugo could just imagine what the result might be if Maggie was let loose with paints and a canvas. The picture would be some kind of abstract——a kaleidoscope of colour and shape that would be vibrant but definitely not restful to have on one's wall. And

Maggie would never attend a painting class as Joan did religiously every Wednesday evening, which precluded any point in issuing an invitation that day.

Thursday provided the most obvious comparison between the personalities of the two women. Not that it was any kind of competition, Hugo reminded himself. It was simply a means of identifying what he was looking for in a partner. A reinforcement of what he knew was the direction he needed to take.

Maggie had hurtled forth, under lights and siren, to bring in a woman who had gone into sudden and unexpected labour at thirty-six weeks into her pregnancy. Marie Jessop had noticed a slight spotting that morning but had called an ambulance when a sudden rush of blood had accompanied an unmistakable contraction. The bleeding had stopped by the time Maggie and Jason delivered Marie to the labour room but the contractions were now five minutes apart.

Joan and Hugo were both concerned about the woman's condition and were disconcerted by the additional family members accompanying the ambulance crew. Marie's four-year-old twin sons, Christopher and Max, were trotting behind the stretcher. Two-year-old Michelle was sitting on her mother's feet.

'We couldn't leave them at home,' Maggie said. 'Dad's a truck driver and is on the road for the day and the neighbour who usually babysits was out.'

Joan had a hospital gown ready for Marie and monitors set up to record the foetal heart rate and uterine contractions. She took the extras in her stride although her tone was slightly resigned.

'Christopher and Max can sit in the waiting room,' she said. 'There's plenty of toys and I'm sure they can look after Michelle until we can find a staff member who's available.'

'No!' the boys said loudly.

Maggie lifted Michelle from the end of the stretcher.

'We want to stay with Mummy,' Max added.

Hugo was helping to transfer Marie to the bed.

'Contractions are five minutes apart,' Maggie told him. 'And Marie's had good effect from breathing entonox. Estimated blood loss was about two hundred mils. Nothing since. Vital signs are all within normal limits.'

'I *told* Dave not to go to Invercargill today.' Marie sounded distressed. 'I just knew something was going to go wrong.'

Maggie took the mouthpiece off the portable entonox cylinder. 'He's on his way back but it'll be an hour or so before he gets here.'

She attached it to the tubing on the large cylinder in the labour room and pressed it into Marie's hand as her agonised expression heralded another contraction. Jason was trying to push the stretcher from the room but was being hampered by the two small boys trying to climb aboard.

'Shell had a ride. We want one, too.'

'Do you want a hand getting Marie into a gown?' Maggie asked Joan.

'No. We'll manage. You could take the children down to the waiting room if you like. That would be a help.'

Marie spat out her mouthpiece. 'Can't they stay here? I don't want them where I can't see them.'

'I'll get the toy box from the waiting room,' Hugo decided. 'They can play in the corner until we get sorted out.'

'I'll get out of the way,' Jason said. He took the entonox cylinder from Maggie. 'I'll sort the gear and get the truck cleaned up.'

'Thanks.' Maggie had the feeling she'd better stick around for a few minutes at least. Joan was not looking pleased at having the children around. She pulled the curtain, screening the bed as she helped Marie into a hospital gown. Christopher stood on tiptoe beside the handbasin on the wall, pulled the handle hard and sent cold water gushing out with enough force to spray both himself and his brother. They both giggled.

'I'll get the toys, shall I?' Maggie offered.

'Thanks.' Hugo wasn't at all sure how to deal with the impending chaos. The last child in a delivery room under his management had been young Henry Cross, and that had been fraught until Joan had taken charge. Marie's midwife had too much on her mind at present to deal with disruptive children and Hugo knew it would be virtually impossible to find any extra staff who weren't busy. They were stretched for nursing cover anyway and Joan hadn't expected to be in for anything other than a check on Monday's new arrivals who needed attention prior to discharge.

An examination showed Marie's labour to be progressing rapidly but normally despite the untoward beginnings, and Hugo was confident that Joan would be able to manage the birth. He was not unduly concerned about the baby's early arrival either but would need to stay in case of any problems. Joan looked less calm than usual, probably because of the distractions in the room. Christopher was playing peek-a-boo with the curtain now and making Michelle shriek with laughter. Max was wriggling under the chair, hoping to catch his mother's attention. He was highly unlikely to be successful.

'I need to push,' Marie gasped. 'I want to sit up more.'

Hugo helped her change position. Joan cast a despairing glance at the children and took action. She pulled Max out from under the chair by his legs and stood him up. She grabbed Christopher's hand and marched both boys to the corner of the room where Maggie had just deposited a large box.

'Sit here quietly and play with the toys,' she ordered. 'If you're good you'll get an ice block.' She leaned down until she was at eye level with the twins. 'If you're not good, you'll get a *smack*.'

Hugo's jaw sagged slightly but fortunately Marie was far too absorbed with what was going on in her body to have overheard the threat, and it certainly had the desired effect on the boys who sat down hurriedly with horrified expressions. Even Michelle co-operated and crawled over to join her brothers. Maggie, who was in the process of pulling some toys from the box, raised an eyebrow as she caught Hugo's glance but said nothing.

The background noise of the children's activity accompanied Marie's next contraction and grew steadily. Michelle was happily hammering at a row of wooden pegs and Max was driving a toy truck up Christopher's back. Joan's face was grim as she stepped away from her patient for a second.

'Could you, *please*, keep them a bit quieter?' she snapped at Maggie.

The next thing Hugo saw was Maggie with Michelle in her arms and a finger to her lips, leading the two boys from the room. They followed with exaggerated tiptoeing steps, their fingers on their own lips and a look of delighted conspiracy on their faces.

For a while, the medical staff all forgot about both the paramedic and the children as they focussed on bringing Marie's new daughter into the world safely. The baby was fine, the third stage of labour quite brief and only some minor stitching was required for Marie. It was as the final stitch was tied that they began wondering what had happened to the rest of Marie's offspring.

'Maggie will be looking after them,' Hugo assured Marie. 'Don't worry. I'll go and see where they've got to.'

Jason was alone in the duty room of the ambulance station. 'I haven't seen her,' he told Hugo. 'And we haven't been paged for another job.' He grinned. 'She could be anywhere—especially if she's got a bunch of kids to play with.'

Hugo went outside to check the small playground on the other side of the outpatient department but there was no sign of anybody. Thinking of the tasks piling up for him in the various wards with increasing urgency made the search irritating. It was just like Maggie to follow through on some plan of her own without considering its impact on others. And it certainly wasn't the first time she had got into trouble with children.

Remembering the sight of the small boys tiptoeing after her from the labour room brought back a more distant memory of the day Maggie had absconded with her whole kindergarten class in tow. Where had she gone that day? Hugo snorted with unamused laughter. She had taken them all home and fed them every scrap of food she could find in her pantry. He changed direction and headed for the hospital kitchens.

Sure enough, there they were. Ethel, the hospital's chief cook, was smiling at the scene in the corner of her domain. Christopher and Max were standing on chairs at a table, stirring something in a large basin. Maggie had Michelle propped on one hip as she upended a box of chocolate chips into the bowl.

'We need lots of chocolate,' Hugo heard her say firmly. 'It's good for you.'

'Only in small doses.'

Maggie's gaze lifted sharply and her delighted grin welcomed Hugo into the small adventure she had provided for the children. She had a dusting of flour on her face. And in her hair and all over the sticky-faced toddler in her arms. No doubt ice blocks had preceded the biscuit-making venture.

'You've got a new sister,' Hugo told the twins. 'And Mummy wants to show her to you.' He raised an eyebrow at Maggie. 'Mummy had no idea where you all were.'

'Oop, sorry.' Maggie rubbed at the flour on her nose. 'We only got the idea to make bikkies after we sneaked in here to find an ice block.'

'We don't want to see Mummy,' Max informed Hugo. 'We want to stay with Maggie.'

Chris nodded solemnly. 'We don't want a smack,' he added.

'You won't get a smack,' Hugo promised. Of course they wouldn't. Joan wouldn't have even made the threat unless she had been under extreme duress. Hugo knew how good Joan was with children. He also knew that she would use any reasonable means to keep order when necessary and that was a positive attribute. Maggie's skills at providing alluring entertainment and being an irresistible ringleader were ideal for a babysitter or maybe an aunt, but imagine her as a mother! Life would be a total circus.

'We need to go back now,' he told the children sternly, 'and visit Mummy. Daddy will be here in a few minutes.'

'We're almost finished.' Maggie was apparently going to take the children's side and undermine Hugo's authority in spite of his sternness. 'How about you go and tell Mummy we'll be in to see her with a cup of tea and a bikkie in half an hour?'

Michelle had a chubby fistful of Maggie's hair. She tugged it and Maggie's nose wrinkled. 'Ouch!' She gave the toddler a quick kiss as she disentangled the small hand. 'We'll be as quick as we can,' she promised Hugo. 'And I'm sure Mummy and Daddy would appreciate a few minutes to themselves.'

Maggie still had traces of flour in her hair when Hugo saw her again late that day. Very late. It had taken so long to catch up with all his other patients that any opportunity to spend time with Joan had been lost. And now Hugo was too tired to even worry that nearly a week had gone by without the first step of his plan being implemented. Tomorrow wouldn't work either because Joan was planning an early departure for her weekend in Dunedin. She had taken down many of her paintings from the hospital walls and intended to deliver them to the gallery owner in person.

She rang Hugo on Friday evening. 'Mum's not very well,' she told him. 'I'm going to stay on for a week or so. I've rung Sue and she's happy to cover for me. We don't have any scheduled deliveries coming up.'

'I hope it's nothing serious.' The break in Joan's routine was unusual enough to be disconcerting. 'Can I help in any way?'

'I'll manage,' Joan assured him. 'I think it's just a bug but it's making her arthritis a lot worse. I want to go to the doctor with her and make sure everything possible's being done.'

'Of course. How did it go at the gallery?'

'It was amazing. He loved the paintings.' Joan hesitated for a moment. 'Would you like to come up to Dunedin next weekend?' she asked. 'The exhibition is going to be opened on Saturday at five o'clock. Lots of people have been invited and it's even going to be advertised in the newspaper. It's really exciting, Hugh.'

'It sounds exciting,' Hugo agreed. 'I'm so pleased for

you, Joan.' He glanced over to where Maggie was lying on the floor in front of the fire, one arm over Lass, the other tickling Tuck's exposed chest. He hadn't managed to send any signals via an invitation to Joan. Maybe accepting one from her was an even better idea. Especially when it would involve an overnight stay.

'Saturday, did you say?' He nodded a second later. 'Sure. I'd love to come.'

CHAPTER EIGHT

SATURDAY'S dawn was advanced well enough to illuminate the heaviest frost of the year so far.

'You're not planning to drive too early, are you?' Maggie took another look from the kitchen window as she put her empty plate and coffee-mug into the sink that Hugo had filled with hot, soapy water. 'The roads will be diabolical.'

'I'll wait till lunchtime,' Hugo nodded. 'It'll only take four hours or so to get to Dunedin. I'll still be in plenty of time for the exhibition opening.'

'Don't worry about anything here. I'll take good care of your family.' Maggie took the crust of toast she had saved from her plate and broke it into three pieces. As usual, the dogs were near her feet and she bent down to scratch Lass's white ear. 'We'll have a good time, won't we, guys?'

Hugo's smile was lopsided. He suspected they would probably have a better time than he would. He rinsed the last of the breakfast dishes. At least he could enjoy a morning at home and a walk before he left. Putting the crockery away, Hugo looked up to see Maggie pulling on her coat and gloves. He shook his head.

'It's too cold out there. Wait for a bit.' Hugo knew from experience that the deceptively warm-looking pink of the first rays of sunshine were not yet nearly enough to touch the sub-zero temperature outside.

'No way. I've never seen a hoar frost before. It might start melting.'

'Not likely. It could hang around for days.'

'But the light's so pretty at the moment.' Maggie jammed a woollen hat on her head, hauling it down to squash her hair into submission. 'Besides, these guys are ready for their walk. See?'

Hugo moved from the kitchen until he could see his three elderly farm dogs waiting patiently by the front door. A surge of renewed youth was apparent when Maggie stepped in their direction. Tails wagged, toenails scraped on the tiled entranceway and Seth even produced a muffled woof of excitement. Maggie laughed and raised the plastic bag she held further out of reach.

'Not for you,' she informed her canine fan club. 'These crusts are for the fish, as you should know by now.'

Hugo smiled as he reached for his own protective clothing. The dogs knew perfectly well they would get a share of the stale crusts. Maggie was a sucker for a soulful stare. And Hugo was a sucker for Maggie's enthusiasm. She was quite right—the light was perfect and what did it matter if they were risking a spot of frostbite? These days, aspects of his life that were familiar enough to be enjoyed with quiet pleasure, tempered with due caution, became somehow charged with a life of their own and had become more exciting than Hugo remembered them ever having been in the past.

Like a hoar frost. He led Maggie up the roadway a little so that she could see its effects on the wire fences, the wild gooseberry and briar rose bushes and the winter skeletons of deciduous trees. The formations of ice crystals glittering in the early light were far more spectacular than Hugo had ever seen. Or was he just looking through Maggie's eyes instead of his own?

'I feel like I'm in the depths of Narnia,' Maggie said in

awe. 'The white witch is about to appear over that hill in her sleigh and turn us to stone with a wave of her wand.'

Hugo just grinned. She'd need a turbo-boost in her wand to deal with the sheer *joie de vivre* Maggie was exuding at present.

'Oh, *look*!' Maggie was open-mouthed now, pointing to a tree branch that appeared festooned with starry white flowers. 'How does it *do* that?'

'Hoar frost accumulates slowly,' Hugo told her. 'Interlocking crystals grow out from a seed. In perfect conditions, like this, they grow into these fern and flower shapes. Look at the fence over there.'

'It looks like a shredded lace curtain hanging from the wires. It's amazing, Hugh.'

'Amazingly cold.' Hugo could feel the tips of his fingers and toes protesting, despite their layers of wool. 'Let's head for the beach and get those fish fed.'

The whisper of a breeze wasn't yet enough to mar the mirrored surface of the lake with ripples. The thin tendrils of mist gave the lake a mystical quality that competed with the magic of the frozen landscape they left behind, and the old wooden jetty near the woolshed was almost as thickly coated with frost as the trees had been.

'Don't go near the edge,' Hugo warned. 'It'll be dangerously slippery.'

'I'll just go as far as the fish,' Maggie nodded. 'Don't worry.'

Feeding trout had never been a habit for Hugo. He wouldn't have thought of doing it from his own jetty but Maggie had been enchanted by the eager schools that were accustomed to being fed by tourists from the main jetty in Queenstown.

'We could do that,' she had suggested to Hugo. 'I'll bet

it wouldn't take long for you to attract a whole bunch of trout.'

It had taken longer than Maggie had anticipated but she had persevered over the last couple of weeks, throwing crumbs of stale bread from the end of the jetty. The first, shy response had been enough of a thrill to reward her efforts and now Maggie triumphantly counted each increase in numbers.

'I can see four...no, six trout!' she called excitedly a minute later.

'Don't go any further out,' Hugo warned. He was watching the dogs who were on the jetty with Maggie, waiting for a crust to drop before it reached the water.

'OK.' Maggie stood carefully in the centre of the wooden platform. She scooped out the last of the bread and hurled it towards the end of the jetty. Only half of the handful made it into the water and the dogs launched themselves to claim the rest.

'Lass!' Hugo shouted. 'Seth, Tuck... Come back here.'

He whistled sharply. Tuck and Seth responded reluctantly but Lass kept going. She planted her paws to brake at the first titbit but it was too close to the end of the jetty and the ancient wood was far too icy. The dog skidded into the misty air and fell into the lake with a splash that echoed in the silence.

'*Lass*!' Maggie yelled. 'Oh, *no*!'

'Maggie!' Hugo's shout was as commanding as he could make it but he knew it was too late. Maggie was headed for disaster just as surely as she had been the time she'd tried to fly with her fairy wings off the back of the sofa. Lass was already swimming the short distance to safety but Maggie couldn't see the dog beneath the slats of the jetty because she was moving too quickly in the opposite direction. Far too quickly for her hiking boots to have any hope of finding purchase on the last few wooden planks. The splash Maggie made as she hit the surface of the lake several feet below was a far larger and more ominous sound than the previous one had been and, with her extra weight augmented by bulky winter clothing, Maggie sank like a stone.

The shock of the icy water temperature transmitted itself as pain to every fibre of Maggie's body and time seemed to stop as she tried to fight her way back to the lake's surface. How could it be taking so long? She knew the lake wasn't that deep—the bottom was always visible on calm days with a startling clarity that allowed the colour of individual stones to be seen. More than once she had imagined throwing herself off the jetty and looking forward to the embrace of cool water on a hot summer's day. She had never imagined trying to swim in winter, however, or weighed down by layers of clothing that now felt as though they were trying to drown her.

As her head broke free Maggie knew the passage of time had been distorted by her fear. She could see Lass paddling furiously back to shore and it must have taken only seconds for her to have covered that distance. She could see Hugo walking into the edge of the lake as well, clearly intent on rescuing her.

'I'm OK,' she shouted. 'Stay there, Hugh. Don't get wet!'

The grim expression on his face indicated that Hugo had no intention of listening. Maggie put her efforts into swimming towards him instead. The intense cold was making it difficult to breathe and she had to pause after only a few strokes, but at least now her feet could touch the bottom. And Hugo hadn't been silly enough to dive in. He was only wet to his thighs so far.

'I'm OK,' Maggie gasped again. 'See?' She walked

through the water using her hands as paddles to increase her momentum. She couldn't say anything more before her teeth began chattering violently. Hugo grabbed her hand as soon as she came close enough and he towed her to the shore. Then the rest of her body followed the lead of her teeth and started shaking so hard that Maggie knew she was in trouble. Hugo caught her as she stumbled. He swung her up into his arms without any apparent effort and didn't pause, turning towards the house and whistling for Lass who was still shaking the water from her shaggy coat. Hugo strode across the pebbles of the beach, carrying Maggie in a grip that felt like steel bars.

'You *idiot*, Maggie,' he said furiously. 'You bloody *idiot*.'

'S-s-s-sorry.' Their movement was stirring the air around them and Maggie could feel the chill factor increase alarmingly. Her hands and feet were completely numb now and it was still difficult to breathe. It took only minutes to reach the safety of the house but Maggie knew her body temperature was still dropping rapidly. She could feel her thought processes slowing and was vaguely bemused when Hugo carried her, dripping, into the hallway and past the door that led to the warmth of the fire.

'W-where…are w-we…going?'

'You're going into a hot shower,' Hugo snapped. He deposited her onto the closed lid of the toilet and reached into the shower cubicle to twist the water mixer. 'That'll be hot in thirty seconds,' he said. 'Get your clothes off and get in there.'

'B-but—'

'No "buts",' Hugo growled. 'Have you *any* idea how cold the water in that lake is? And then you get out into sub-zero air temperature. You're probably seriously hypothermic already.'

Maggie held up her arms, the sodden gloves covering hands that no longer functioned. 'B-but, Hugh,' she stuttered, ' I…c-can't.'

The sound Hugo made could have been a groan. It might have been a curse but Maggie couldn't have cared less. She wasn't even embarrassed as Hugo patiently peeled off her clothing, item by item. Her toes looked dead, bloodlessly white with the bright nail polish she hadn't taken off after the fancy-dress ball decorating the tips with blood-red splashes. The wet denim of her jeans scraped her legs painfully and then joined the pile of boots, socks, jacket and jersey. Hugo's own hands seemed too cold to deal with the tiny buttons of her shirt and Maggie felt a ridiculous urge to giggle as she saw them ping free and scatter on the tiles. Then Hugo was pulling her to her feet and pointing her through the clouds of steam towards the shower cubicle.

'Get in,' he ordered. 'It doesn't matter about your underwear. Stay in there until you feel warm.'

The rain of heat was initially unbearable as Maggie's feet and hands came agonisingly back to life. Then it was wonderful and Maggie just stood there, basking in the warmth until her fingers were mobile enough to undo the catch on her bra and find the edge of elastic on her knickers. She discarded the wet items on the floor of the shower.

'You OK?' Hugo was calling from the other side of the open bathroom door.

'I'm fine,' Maggie called back.

'Get out and get dry,' Hugo instructed. 'I've put your electric blanket on. You'd better go back to bed until you're properly warmed up.'

It sounded like a wonderful idea to Maggie. The effect of reheating the surface of her body on top of the deep chilling and the fright she'd had was giving her a curious and overwhelming lassitude. Wrapped in fluffy towels, Maggie staggered down the hallway towards her bedroom barely able to keep her eyes open. They were actually closed when she felt Hugo grip her arms.

'Come on, then. Into bed.' The corner of the duvet was turned back and the pillows looked soft and inviting. 'Where are your pyjamas?'

'Don't have any,' Maggie mumbled. She pulled the towel from around her body and half fell into her bed, her head still swathed in another towel.

Hugo drew in a sharp breath as he pulled the duvet up to cover Maggie. If he'd had any belief that he was in control of his body's reaction to this woman, the sight of those slim, pale legs and her small, firm breasts had shattered it. The final straw was those cheerful scarlet toenails that brought an instant image of Maggie looking like a naughty harem escapee. He had to get out of this room but he couldn't leave until he was sure Maggie was all right. And he didn't *want* to leave anyway, damn it!

The softness and warmth of the bed were heavenly. Only one thing could make it better as far as Maggie was concerned. She reached up and caught Hugo's hand as he pulled the duvet over her shoulder.

'Come to bed with me, Hugh,' she murmured drowsily.

'Maggie!'

'You're cold, too. Look—you haven't even taken your wet jeans off.'

'I will in a minute. I was getting Lass dried off.'

'Do it now.' The aftermath of the disastrous dip seemed to have tipped Maggie into a state where she didn't care if Hugo knew how she felt about him. She *wanted* him to know and, above all, she wanted him to feel the same way. Nothing else mattered at that moment. 'Please, Hugh,'

Maggie's teeth were chattering again and the words came out as a stutter. 'I n-need you.'

She did need him. Hugo could see that in her face. And when he thought about it she must have had a dreadful fright, falling into that icy lake. She needed some emotional warmth just as much as anything physical, and who better to give her a comforting cuddle than himself? Besides, Maggie was right. He needed to get his wet jeans off. His legs were frozen.

'Just for a minute, then. Until my legs warm up.'

Maggie watched his fingers fumble with the stud on his jeans and then open the zip and peel the stiff fabric away from his skin. This was perfect! The drowsiness was being fired through with tendrils of excitement now. She had had so many dreams like this. Could it be that they were actually going to come true? The icy skin on Hugo's legs had never been part of any fantasy but this reality was so much better. Somehow Maggie had known just how perfectly she would fit, snuggled against Hugo's body, with her head in the hollow of his shoulder and his arm holding her so close. She closed her eyes in sheer bliss and let her hand travel up beneath the shirt Hugo hadn't removed yet.

Hugo gritted his teeth as he felt Maggie's fingers brush his bare skin. Her hands still felt cold which was why his nipple hardened so convulsively even before she touched it. Then he used his free hand to capture hers. Who was he trying to kid?

And what the hell had he been thinking of to torture himself in quite this fashion? He wanted Maggie so badly. The prospect of being able to hold her like this under the guise of providing a bit of extra body warmth and some brotherly comfort had been too tempting an opportunity to resist, but now he realised he might well have bitten off far more than he could chew.

'This is nice, Hugh,' Maggie murmured.

'Mmm.' The response was somewhat strangled and Hugo kept a firm grasp on Maggie's hand. He had better make damned sure it didn't stray in any new direction or Maggie would discover only too easily just how 'nice' his body was finding the experience. Why had he put himself here again? Oh…yes. 'You're quite safe now, Maggie,' Hugo said comfortingly. 'Are you feeling any warmer yet?'

'I feel a bit weird,' Maggie admitted.

'In what way?'

'Kind of sleepy.'

'That's only to be expected. You've had a nasty fright and a period of hypothermia. A good sleep is just what you need.'

'But I don't feel *tired*,' Maggie said. 'That's what's weird. I feel…excited.'

Hugo gritted his teeth hard enough to make his jaw ache as he felt Maggie's move to snuggle even closer. Every cell of his body seemed attuned to hers and was currently shrieking in delight at the situation he'd engineered. Excitement barely scratched the descriptive surface here. He had to get away before he did something they would both regret. Hugo tried to inch away but the best he could persuade his reluctant body to generate was a general tightening of his muscles.

Maggie felt his body tense. 'You're not going yet, are you, Hugh? I'm still cold,' she added unconvincingly.

'This might not be the best way to warm you up.'

Maggie managed to free her hand. She used it to trace Hugo's ribs and then curl around his waist to try and pull him towards her. 'I think it would be a great way to warm up,' she whispered.

Hugo had to summon every ounce of strength he had to

fight this new temptation. But fight it he must. Maggie wasn't herself at present. The physical and mental state she was in was probably comparable to being extremely drunk. And it was so like her to hurl herself into some new adventure or experience without giving the consequences any thought. Thank goodness he had already given the matter quite enough thought for both of them.

'We have too much between us, Maggie,' he said carefully. 'Too many memories. Too much friendship and…love to risk ruining it all by throwing sex into the equation.' He took Maggie's hand and directed it away from his body. 'Not that I'm not tempted,' he added gently. 'But it's not just us that it could hurt, is it?'

'Isn't it?' Maggie tried to focus on what Hugo was saying but it was hard to get past the fact that he was rejecting her. She was hurt already, damn it. Who else did she have to worry about? Donald? Donald meant nothing. He never would.

'There's Joan,' Hugo reminded her. Or was he reminding himself? Using the stab of guilt that he hadn't even thought of Joan as an obstacle until he'd been desperate. The guilt was tempered by a wave of gratitude that she was available. He could protect Maggie from herself now. And from him. The existence of another woman in his life was clearly enough to bring Maggie back to her senses.

'Ah…yes. So there is.' Maggie's body seemed to be shrinking. Drawing into itself. The movement prompted Hugo to remove his enfolding arm and Maggie let her head flop onto the pillow. 'Sorry, Hugh.' She shut her eyes. 'Forget I said anything.'

'Consider it forgotten.' Hugh had the opportunity he needed to escape but even now his body was considering rebellion. 'Are you warm enough now, Maggie?'

'I'm fine.' Maggie's eyes were firmly shut now. 'I think I'll go to sleep for a bit.'

'Good idea.' Hugo finally managed to force his body to move. The air felt astonishingly cold against his bare legs as he left the warmth of the bed. Something deep inside Hugo felt even colder. He stooped to pick up his wet jeans and then hesitated yet again.

'Still friends, Maggie?'

'Of course,' Maggie said wearily. She rolled, turning her face away from him. 'Still friends, Hugh.'

The dousing had the effect of subduing Maggie for days.

'Are you sure you're OK? You're not brewing up pneumonia or something, are you?'

'I'm fine.' Maggie was stuffing folders into a rucksack. 'I won't be home for dinner tonight. I'm starting the new volunteer induction course. We have a two-hour lecture between seven and nine so I'll just stay and work and catch up on the stock-take or something.'

'Didn't you finish that last night?'

'No. By the time I got back from that call to Wanaka it was too late to do much.' Maggie was looking around the living area. 'Have you seen my boots anywhere?'

'They're under the table.'

'Thanks.' Maggie's grin had a flash of her normal exuberance. 'I'm a messy creature, aren't I? Must be horrible for someone as tidy as you to have around.'

'I like having you around.' It was the closest reference in days to the supposedly forgotten exchange they'd had when Maggie had invited Hugo to her bed. The awkward pause that followed was quite enough for them both to acknowledge the unlikelihood of forgetting a single word of that conversation. Maggie pulled on her boots with determined movements.

'Is Joan coming back today?'

'It didn't sound like it when I spoke to her yesterday. Her mother seems to be getting worse rather than better.'

'I still need to apologise.'

'I already did that. She understands that I couldn't make it to the exhibition opening.'

'You didn't really need to stay. I could have looked after myself.'

'Hmm.'

It was a noncommittal sound and Maggie sighed. She hadn't looked after herself very well in the first place, had she? If Hugo hadn't been there when she'd fallen into the lake she could have been in real trouble. No wonder he thought of her as immature and irresponsible. No wonder Joan was a far more attractive proposition as an equal partner. Maggie had never stood a chance and now Hugo was being so considerate, carrying on as though nothing had changed. As though his home and his protection was as available as it had ever been. But the change was undeniable and Maggie had come to the conclusion that it was time she demonstrated some maturity.

'I've decided I will take that room in Jason's flat.' Maggie was trying to sound mature and practical but the words came out sounding too high-pitched. Almost defensive. She cleared her throat and tried again. 'I'm going to move in on Friday.'

'Are you sure that's what you want to do?'

Maggie couldn't meet his gaze. Of course she didn't want to but she couldn't suffer any more like this either, being so close to Hugo. Loving him this much…and knowing he would never feel the same way. It was obvious that having her around had become uncomfortable. They had been so careful around each other since Saturday. Four days of determinedly casual contact when it had been too pointed to continue their mutual avoidance tactics. Like when Hugo had finally returned home on Sunday after so much time in his office 'catching up' on paperwork. Or when Maggie had stayed on station on Monday evening to sort out all the training materials she needed for the induction course.

The tension Maggie had been aware of for weeks was now there for both of them but the cause was so sadly different. Maggie loved Hugo. She wanted him. Hugo also loved Maggie but he didn't want her. He was too kind to spell it out and she was too embarrassed and disappointed to want him to.

'Of course it's what I want. It'll be great.' Maggie managed a much more upbeat tone this time. 'It'll be fun. Lots of parties, I expect.'

Hugo nodded. 'You'll enjoy that.'

'Absolutely.' The smile Maggie had summoned felt dangerously wobbly. She turned away, disguising the threat of tears by giving the dogs an extra farewell cuddle.

It did the trick. Maggie swallowed her tears and gathered her new maturity around her like a cloak. She could handle this.

She *had* to.

It became easier by tinier degrees after the wrench of moving out of the lakeside house. And it had the advantage of making any other hassles in her life appear relatively insignificant and easy to cope with. What did it matter that her new lifestyle was messy and noisy and lacking in privacy? The distraction was a bonus, in fact. Even dealing with Donald when he arrived for his cardiology outpatient clinic that week was easy.

'No, I don't want to have lunch with you, Donald,'

Maggie said crisply. 'I don't really think that your wife would be very happy about that, would she?'

'We're separated, I told you that.'

'Somebody else told me something a little different.'

'Oh? Who said that?'

'I would have thought that what mattered was whether it was true or not, rather than who said it.'

Donald was silent for a moment. 'OK, I'll be honest with you, Maggie. I *am* still living with my wife but it's not going to last. We've had problems. We still do.'

'I'm not surprised,' Maggie said coolly. 'But if you have any intention of adding me to the list of problems, you can forget it, Donald. I'm not interested.'

She wasn't interested. And it seemed to Maggie that she would never be interested in another man for as long as she lived. She already knew that nobody existed who matched the ideal she had woven around her memories of Hugo Patterson. Now that she knew the attraction of the real man was infinitely more powerful than that blueprint, she had no intention of even trying to locate a substitute. She would only be doomed to failure and disappointment.

The cheerful companionship of her new flatmates was welcome but barely touched the emptiness that Hugo's absence left in her life. It had been less than a week since she'd moved out and Maggie had never seen that much of Hugo during her working days so the constant awareness of missing him was unexpected. And dealing with it was harder than Maggie had anticipated. By Thursday night she was tired. The late call that came in was unwelcome.

'Not Dulcie Payne again,' Jason groaned. 'Why doesn't he lock the doors?'

'She's been missing for over an hour,' Maggie sighed. 'The police are worried that she'll be hypothermic by the time they find her. They want us on standby in town.'

'We'll end up searching for her ourselves,' Jason warned. 'The last time she went missing she'd decided that someone's potting shed was where she'd lived all her life. They had an awful job finding her and that was in daylight.'

'Let's hope it's quicker this evening, then. And let's grab an extra foil sheet from the storeroom in case it isn't.' Maggie pulled herself to her feet. 'We'll put a bag of IV fluids on the dash so that the heater warms it up. That'll be the best way to warm her quickly if she is in trouble.'

It was nearly eight o'clock by the time Dulcie Payne was located, lying in the cemetery near the motor camp. She had fallen, giving herself a Colles' fracture of her wrist and she was also dangerously cold. Maggie and Jason wrapped the frail old woman in a foil sheet and then covered her with blankets. Jason splinted her wrist while Maggie struggled with finding IV access on her other arm. Tom Payne sat on the spare stretcher, wheezing heavily as he watched the crew working.

'It's my fault,' he said, yet again. 'I let her go to the toilet by herself and she just wandered out the back door.'

'She's going to be fine,' Maggie said reassuringly. 'This warm fluid will bring her body temperature up quite quickly.' She eyed Tom as she hooked up the giving set. 'I'm going to give you some Ventolin,' she decided. 'And some oxygen. You're having a bit more trouble than usual with your breathing, aren't you?'

'It gets worse…when I'm worried. I don't know what…I'm going to do.'

Tom's breathing had improved by the time they reached the hospital but Maggie stayed with both her patients until Hugo and Lizzie had checked Dulcie thoroughly and then taken her for an X-ray. She was still sitting with Tom when

Hugo came back. He sat down beside them with a serious expression on his face.

'We'll put a cast on that wrist and make sure Dulcie's completely warmed up,' he told Tom. 'She's going to recover from this but it's time we talked about the future, Tom. You can't go on like this. Either of you.'

'I'm not going to put her in a home.' Tears filled the elderly man's eyes and Maggie took his hand in hers and squeezed it.

'It's OK, Tom,' she said softly. 'We do understand how difficult this is. You love Dulcie and you want to do the best for her.'

Tom nodded. He sniffed noisily and pulled a large handkerchief from his pocket with his free hand.

'And Dulcie loves you, even though she might not remember it most of the time,' Maggie continued softly. 'She would want what's best for you as well, wouldn't she?'

'She always put me first,' Tom said brokenly. 'Always looked after me. Sixty years we've been together. We were never blessed with any children so it's only ever been the two of us. I'm not going to let anyone split us up.'

'Nobody wants to do that, Tom.'

'And there could be a different way to manage this,' Maggie suggested. She turned to Hugo. 'Are there any of those retirement villages in the area? The ones with the staged care?'

'There's a new facility that's been built in Frankton. Independent units with staff available from the rest home when they're needed. They've built it close to the hospital so that the on-call doctor will always be available and they'll have access to the long-stay geriatric beds as back up.'

'They'd have larger units for married couples, wouldn't they?'

Hugo nodded. 'It's terribly expensive, though,' he warned. 'Especially with the kind of extra care Dulcie would need.'

'I've got money,' Tom said.

Hugo and Maggie exchanged a surprised glance. The Paynes lived in a modest house with few obvious luxuries.

'I could have, anyway.' Tom had intercepted the glance. 'Have you seen the view from our old house? I've been offered nearly a million dollars for the section alone. I've always told the developers to go away. There was no way I'd make Dulcie leave her home. We've lived there since the day we were married.' He sighed heavily. 'But she doesn't even remember it *is* her home, does she? She seems to spend half her life trying to escape.'

'Having a lovely place to live in is wonderful,' Maggie said, 'but it's *who* you live with that really matters. Would you be prepared to sell your home if it meant that you and Dulcie could stay together? Safely?'

'I guess I could have a look at the place,' Tom said cautiously after a long pause. 'And see if it's good enough for Dulcie.'

'Would you like me to come with you? I've seen a lot of these places, working as an ambulance officer. I know what to look for and what questions to ask.'

The two men stood watching when Maggie left a few minutes later, having made an arrangement for such a visit the next day. Tom was smiling for the first time since he'd arrived at the hospital.

'What a lovely girl she is. Reminds me of my Dulcie…sixty years ago, that is.'

Hugo just nodded. He was still a little stunned by Maggie's sensitive and compassionate handling of the case and her ability to find a solution that now seemed so simple. He had been even more struck by the comment she'd made that who you lived with was more important than where you lived.

Hugo lived in the most beautiful spot on earth but since Maggie had moved out it had felt different.

It felt like the emptiest spot on earth.

CHAPTER NINE

'JOAN! It's so good to see you.'

'It's good to see you too, Hugh.'

'I was beginning to think you were never coming back.'

'Why don't you sit down?' Joan stepped away from Hugo's hug. 'I'll make us some coffee. Or would you prefer wine?'

'Coffee would be great. It's been a long day.' Hugo knew his smile was probably strained. This was it. He had come to the realisation that there was no way on earth his future could contain a closer relationship with Joan and it was unacceptable to let things dangle any longer. Hugo didn't like letting people down and he didn't want to destroy the friendship he had with Joan, but the unpleasant necessity remained and this was the first opportunity Hugo had had to speak to her face to face. He was momentarily distracted from his preoccupation over how to achieve this mission as kindly as possible by having to move a box from the cream couch to give himself room to sit down.

'You must have brought a lot of stuff back with you. It almost looks as though you're packing up.'

'I am.' Joan placed a steaming mug on the coffee-table with deliberation. 'We need to talk, Hugh.'

Indeed they did. Hugo was a little worried by the frown of concern on Joan's face. Had she guessed why he had come to see her tonight? Or was something else about to take priority over the subject he wanted to raise?

'Are you still worried about your mother? Have you decided you do need to live closer?'

'Yes.' Joan sat down carefully, leaving a noticeable gap between herself and her guest. 'But I wasn't being entirely honest with you when we talked last night.'

'Oh?' It hadn't been a long conversation as Hugo remembered, and he'd done most of the talking, but it had been perfectly friendly. While the decision to put an end to any hopes Joan might have of their relationship going further had already been made, it was not a conversation Hugo had considered fair to conduct over the phone. He couldn't think of anything less than truthful Joan might have said. Mind you, the call hadn't done much to alleviate that empty feeling at home. He had called his mother almost immediately for a much longer chat, and a long conversation with Gwen Patterson could leave anyone feeling forgetful.

'You mean your mother isn't that unwell?'

'No, that's not what I meant.'

'Oh.' Hugo tried to recall the other subjects they'd talked about. He had told Joan that the new ventilator had arrived for the emergency department and how pleased they all were. He'd shared the pleasure of Tom Payne's decision to move into the retirement village with Dulcie and how well Charlie Barker was doing now that he was back home after his cardiac surgery. He'd commented on the sadness he felt now that Nancy was failing so fast and he'd even admitted that it felt lonely living by himself now that Maggie had moved out. Joan had sounded unexpectedly sympathetic that he was missing Maggie's company. Was that what she had been less than honest about?

Joan's face was screened by a curtain of blonde hair and it took Hugo a second or two to realise that it wasn't just the three-week absence that was making her seem so unfamiliar. Thank goodness he'd noticed before having to be told.

'You're wearing your hair loose,' he said. 'It looks great.'

'Thanks.' Joan turned to meet Hugo's gaze. She hesitated for a long moment and her words were tentative when she finally spoke again. 'We're friends, aren't we, Hugh?'

'Of course. Good friends.'

'And friends *should* be honest with each other, shouldn't they?'

'Of course,' Hugo said again. He found himself speaking as cautiously as Joan seemed to be doing. Hugo had the uncomfortable feeling he was about to be taken to task for his less than enthusiastic approach to their relationship. And justifiably so. Maybe Joan had used her absence to contemplate their future and had made a similar decision to the one Hugo had so recently embraced. That it was time to test their relationship with a 'make or break' scenario. Except that Hugo understood now that they would never 'make' it and it would be totally unfair to them both to even try. But Hugo was still reluctant to hurt her. His mouth went a little dry and he gripped the handle of his coffee-mug more firmly.

'We've never been more than good friends, though, have we?'

'I always thought we could be,' Hugo said slowly. He didn't want Joan to think he had simply been toying with her emotions. 'Given time.'

'I thought that, too.' Joan's smile was poignant. 'I spent a long time hoping that something would happen between us.' Her obvious regret was contagious.

'I'm very fond of you, Joan,' Hugo said quietly. 'And I have the greatest admiration for your achievements. I'm really sorry I couldn't make it for your exhibition opening.'

'That doesn't matter.' Joan shook her head, dismissing the apology as irrelevant. 'The thing is, Hugh…we're not in love, are we?'

'No.' Being honest was not as difficult as Hugo had anticipated but it was sad just the same. His smile was lopsided. 'We really like each other, though, don't we?'

Joan's smile was fleeting. 'Liking someone isn't enough,' she said quietly. 'Maybe a lot of people think it is and they end up with a long and successful marriage but I think that would be a bit sad. Compared to the real thing, it might even seem boring.' Joan met Hugo's glance again. 'I *thought* I might be in love with you,' she continued. 'But now I know I wasn't.'

'How can you be so sure?' The look he caught shining in the depths of Joan's pale eyes answered the question all by itself and Hugo found himself smiling again as he nodded his understanding. 'You're in love with someone else.'

'Yes.'

'Lewis Evans?'

Joan nodded. 'I didn't mean it to happen, Hugh. I wasn't looking for anyone else. I guess it started the night of the ball. Or maybe even before that, when he was so taken with my paintings that day. Nothing happened,' she added quickly. 'At least not until the exhibition opening. He could see I was disappointed that you hadn't been able to make it and he took me out for dinner afterwards. And…and that's what I wasn't being honest about. It's not just my mother who wants me to go back to Dunedin to live. Lewis has asked me to marry him and I've said yes.'

'Congratulations.' There didn't seem much more that Hugo could say really. 'I hope you'll be very happy together.'

'I know we will.' Joan reached out and squeezed Hugo's hand briefly. 'You'll find someone too, Hugh. You'll fall in love and then you'll know that what we had wasn't anything like the real thing.'

Hugo was silent. He should be feeling relieved, he thought. Joan had taken the initiative and achieved exactly what he had come here to achieve. They had sorted out their relationship and Joan was not wounded or even upset. In fact, Hugo had never seen her look happier and maybe that was what was causing the odd reaction he was having. He felt…envious. Joan had found the real thing. It would never seem boring. She had found the kind of bond that had welded Charlie and Betty Barker together. Or Tom and Dulcie Payne. Something that could last and even grow stronger over a lifetime.

Hugo managed to push the envy aside. 'I'll keep an eye out for the real article,' he said lightly. 'And hope that I recognise it.'

'Oh, you will,' Joan said confidently. 'You'll find you don't want to be away from that person for a minute longer than you need to be. You'll think about them all the time and miss them whenever you're not together.'

Hugo was missing Maggie. He spent a lot of his time thinking about her.

'They'll make you laugh even when what they say isn't funny to anyone else.'

Maggie made him laugh. There had been more laughter around him in the few weeks they had lived together than Hugo could ever remember. Apart from those years of Maggie and Felicity being together, of course.

'And taking things slowly simply isn't an option when you want to touch somebody that badly,' Joan added softly.

Hugo sighed. He knew whom he had wanted to touch that badly. And still did.

'You won't have to look very far, you know.' Joan was smiling again. 'Maggie loves you.'

'I'm a big brother as far as Maggie's concerned,' Hugo said flatly. 'Of course she loves me. And I love her. But it's not *that* kind of love.' The echo of his words prompted a mental image of Maggie lying in the nest of her duvet and pillows and her sleepy acceptance of his gentle rejection.

'Isn't it?' Joan raised an eyebrow. 'I've seen the way Maggie looks at you, Hugh. I was jealous without realising quite why, but now I know. I know how I feel when I look at Lewis and I know that the way Maggie feels about you has nothing to do with being part of a family. She's *not* your sister, Hugh. And she doesn't want to be.'

'It could never work.' Hugo shook his head firmly. 'Maggie would drive me nuts. She's untidy and often irresponsible and even reckless occasionally.' His smile was wry. 'She's frankly naughty sometimes. Like a big kid.'

'So maybe she needs someone like you around.'

'Maybe she does.' Hugo smiled as he made a move to leave Joan's apartment, although he knew his portrayal of Maggie as still being a child was not the whole picture. She was quite capable of being as responsible and professional as he was when she needed to be, and she was funny and courageous and fascinating as well. She was just… Maggie. 'And maybe we'll find out one day.'

'I know you will.' Joan followed Hugo to the door and gave him a hug. 'Still friends, Hugh?'

'Of course, Joan. Still friends.'

Hugo walked the short distance to where his Jeep was parked. The temptation to believe what Joan had suggested was very strong. Almost as irresistible as the impulse that had led Hugo to climb into Maggie's bed that day. And maybe Joan was right. It had been Maggie's invitation after all that had provided the opportunity to hold her that closely. One that could, so easily, have led to more. He had used Joan as a shield on that occasion, thinking that he was protecting both himself and Maggie. And Maggie had accepted it. By tomorrow, however, Joan's engagement was likely to be common knowledge around the hospital and Maggie would know that the shield was no longer there. There was nothing to stop them getting closer.

Not if that was something they *both* wanted.

Hugo slowed the Jeep more judiciously than was really needed as he approached the intersection. The new temptation was to turn and drive into Queenstown instead of the opposite direction that would take him home. He could go and see Maggie right now. It would be risky. Maggie might back off and the foundations of their friendship could be irretrievably shaken, but if Joan was right then the risk was more than well worth taking.

But what if Joan was wrong? It had been Maggie's confused and drowsy state that had prompted the invitation to her bed. It hadn't been even hinted at since. Other memories flicked in to provide further warning. He was the same age as her previous lover—the boring hunk. He was mature. And safe. And Maggie had made it very clear that she didn't want someone who might try to tone her down. She had moved out of his home. How could that be interpreted as anything other than a signal that she wanted more, rather than less, distance between them?

And it was late. Just how did he intend to pass off an unannounced visit at this time of night with her flatmates as a curious audience? It wasn't as if he and Maggie were spending any real time together at present. Hugo hadn't even seen or spoken to Maggie in three days now and leaping into a conversation of this nature without giving Maggie any warning would be unfair.

More than unfair. Allowing impatience or sheer desire to rule his approach might undermine any chance of success. With a heartfelt sigh, Hugo pulled the steering-wheel of the Jeep to the right and let his headlights illuminate the way home. Tomorrow, he promised himself. Tomorrow he would find a way to talk to Maggie.

It had been three days since Maggie had seen Hugo. She kept hoping that the few calls they got in that time would be to patients who would need transporting to the emergency department of the hospital but they were frustratingly easy to deal with where they were. A person confined to a wheelchair had fallen and, although uninjured, had required the assistance of the ambulance service to get mobile again. A diabetic who normally managed his condition well needed IV glucose after a collapse but they declined transport to hospital and his family was quite happy to monitor him at home.

At the second minor car accident they attended, Maggie tried to persuade a woman with seat-belt bruising that a check-up at the local hospital might be prudent before continuing her journey. She was getting desperate for an excuse to get into the hospital but it needed to be work-related. She couldn't just bounce in and congratulate Joan on her surprise engagement to Lewis Evans when she'd only heard about it that morning. Or corner Hugo to see if he was upset about the unexpected development in his life. Unfortunately, the accident victim wasn't impressed by her persuasive efforts.

'I've waited too long for this holiday already. I'm not going to waste a minute of it sitting in some hospital waiting room.'

'It's quite a nasty bruise.'

'I'll probably have a few more by the time I've been

skiing for a week. Look, it's nice of you to be concerned but I'm fine. If it gets any worse I'll go and see a doctor.'

The call to a young baby late that afternoon felt far more significant. Recognising the address, Maggie drove full tilt to the Jessops' house. Marie's baby daughter was less than a month old and as an experienced mother of four, Marie was not likely to call an ambulance for anything minor. Catching sight of Jason's face after a rapid manoeuvre through heavy traffic on the open road was almost amusing.

It reminded Maggie of Hugo's expression when she'd driven him to Charlie Barker's. Fortunately, the loud wail of the siren covered Jason's fervent oath.

Marie was apologetic at having called an ambulance. 'Sorry, Maggie, but I didn't know what to do. The doctor said to bring her in to the medical centre but I have to wait for my neighbour to come and look after the other kids and I'm really not happy about Lucy.'

Two-year-old Michelle was toddling towards Maggie with a huge smile on her face and her arms extended. The twins, Christopher and Max, had also spotted their visitors.

'Bikkies!' they shouted. 'Let's make bikkies!'

'Not today,' Maggie said sadly. She ruffled the twins' matching dark curls. 'I've come to see Lucy this time.' She turned back to Marie and the grizzling baby she held in her arms. 'What's been happening?'

Ten minutes later, the neighbour arrived to care for the older children and Maggie was in the back of the ambulance with Marie and Lucy on the way to hospital.

'Couldn't we just go to the medical centre?'

Maggie shook her head. 'I think Lucy might need more tests and treatment than they could manage. There's nothing obvious that could be causing her fever and, like you, I don't feel happy about the way she is. You can't be too careful with tiny babies like Lucy. And I've told the hospital we're on our way now. Hugh will be expecting us.'

Maggie met Hugo's gaze as she helped Marie from the back of the ambulance. For a split second she thought that he was experiencing the same sharp jolt of pleasure as seeing him had given her, but the moment was gone too quickly as Hugo's attention focussed on the mother of his new patient.

'Marie!' His arm went around her shoulders as he guided her towards the assessment room. He was looking at the baby in her arms as they walked. 'What's been happening with Lucy?'

'She's been really fussy since early this morning. She's not feeding well. She's crying a lot and she seems floppy.'

Hugo looked up at Maggie who was walking on Marie's other side.

'Lucy has a temperature of 39.5. She's tachycardic at 174 beats per minute. Her airway's clear but she's in mild respiratory distress with sternal retractions and a respiration rate of 60. Her lung fields are clear. No rashes or petechiae and no vomiting or diarrhoea.'

'Anyone else sick in the family at the moment?' Hugo queried. 'How are the twins? And Michelle?'

Lizzie was tucking a clean sheet over the bed in the resuscitation area. She greeted Marie warmly but the young mother responded with only a distracted smile as she answered Hugo.

'Someone's always got a runny nose or a cough in our house. Nothing major. Is it an ear infection, do you think? Max had one when he was only three months old.' Marie bit her lip. 'It couldn't be meningitis, could it, Hugh?'

'We'll have a good look at her. You sit up on the bed here and hold Lucy. It'll be less upsetting for her that way.'

'Mind if I stay?' Maggie asked. 'I'm nearly off duty

now and I'm curious to see what you find. I might have missed something I shouldn't have.'

'Please, do.' Hugo smiled. It was a brief invitation that Marie echoed but the smile stayed with Maggie for several minutes as she watched him.

She had almost forgotten the way Hugo's eyes crinkled when he smiled and the way he moved and spoke with such measured confidence and skill. He was handling baby Lucy so gently that Maggie had to swallow the lump that came to her throat. She was missing Hugo far more than she had even realised.

'She's running quite a fever,' Hugo said a few minutes later. 'And she certainly seems off colour. Her ears are fine, chest is clear and I can't find anything amiss with her tummy. She's a little pale with slightly delayed capillary refill but no rashes.'

'So it's not meningitis?'

'We'll do some tests to exclude it properly but there are no real signs of it,' Hugo told Marie. 'Her neck's not stiff and she doesn't mind the light in her eyes and, as Maggie noticed, there's no sign of any rash.'

'I would have got us here a lot faster if there had been,' Maggie said.

Hugo grinned at Marie. 'And you wouldn't have enjoyed that. Maggie's a fiend when the siren's on.' The glance Maggie received was affectionate enough to spark a warmth that threatened to turn into a blush.

Marie hadn't noticed the glance. 'The boys wanted her to stay and make biscuits.'

Maggie was trying to divert her blush. She reached out and touched the top of Lucy's head gently. 'She's not showing signs of real dehydration, is she?'

'Not yet. The fontanelle's normal. With this temperature and respiration rate, along with her reduced feeding, I think we should definitely start fluids, though, and we need IV access anyway for blood samples.'

'What for?' Marie asked anxiously.

'It looks like Lucy has a generalised infection of some kind.'

Maggie was nodding. 'Neonatal sepsis,' she murmured. 'Marie did have perinatal complications with that bleeding.'

'And Lucy was a few weeks early,' Hugo added. 'They're both factors for increased risk of neonatal sepsis.'

'What's causing the infection?' Marie asked anxiously.

'We don't know yet. We're going to need to take a throat swab and some blood and urine samples. We'll have to do a lumbar puncture as well so we can be absolutely sure it's not meningitis.'

'A lumbar puncture!' Marie's face paled. 'But that's awful.'

'It's not too bad,' Hugo said gently. 'It involves using a tiny needle in Lucy's back to take a sample of the spinal fluid. We'll use some local anaesthetic so it won't hurt her very much. It's an important test, Marie, and if we find where this infection is then we'll know exactly what sort of antibiotics we need to get on top of it.'

'I don't think I could watch that, Hugh, I'm sorry.'

'You don't have to.' Hugo turned to his nurse. 'Lizzie, could you take Marie down to the kitchens and make her a cup of tea? Give Steve a call and make sure he stays to keep the lab open for these tests and you might like to give Dave a ring and let him know what's happening. Tell him we'll probably need to keep Marie and Lucy in hospital for a day or two.'

'Oh, no! Why?'

'We need to start Lucy on antibiotics and the quickest way for them to be effective is to give them intravenously.

We'll use a broad cover until we can identify exactly what sort of bug we're dealing with but I'll be waiting for the test results in case we need to change things and they may take a few hours to come through.' Hugo gave Marie's shoulder a reassuring squeeze. 'Lucy's not feeding well and she's losing body fluids by having a high temperature and fast breathing rate. We'll have to give her replacement fluids intravenously as well.'

'But we can stay here? You're not going to send us away somewhere like Invercargill?'

'Only if Lucy shows any signs of getting worse in the next few hours. If that does happen we'll be sending you straight off to a specialist.'

'Dave will never cope.'

'I'm sure he will.' Lizzie had her arm around Marie who was now looking thoroughly frightened. 'Come on, we'll go and talk to him.' She raised an eyebrow as Marie reluctantly handed her baby over to Hugo. 'You're going to need some help with these tests.'

'Maggie trained as a nurse before she became a paramedic. She's probably better than I am at finding IV access.' Hugo's gaze shifted. 'Is that OK, Maggie? Can you stay a bit longer and give me a hand?'

'Sure. I'm officially off duty now.' Maggie realised that Hugo could just as easily have asked her to keep Marie company elsewhere instead of Lizzie. She was quite confident Hugo could manage whatever invasive procedures were needed but if he was using her skills as an excuse to keep her around then Maggie was more than happy to oblige. 'I'd love to help.' She smiled at Marie. 'I was a paediatric nurse for quite a while. Don't worry, we'll take very good care of Lucy.'

Taking blood samples and doing a lumbar puncture on a three-and-a-half-week-old baby took time and all the skill that both Hugo and Maggie possessed. It was a focussed and, at times, tense period that precluded any kind of personal exchange, and it wasn't until baby Lucy had been settled in the medical ward under the care of her mother and Megan with full antibiotic cover started and fluid replacement under way that either of them could relax.

'You deserve a coffee,' Hugo told Maggie. 'Have you got time?'

'Sure.' It was hard to keep her tone light. This was the opportunity Maggie had been hoping for to spend some time alone with Hugo. Of course she had time. If she hadn't, she would have created it out of thin air. Maggie walked away from the ward with Hugo by her side and found she had to take a deep breath to cope with a new— and odd—sense of trepidation. Hugo had been delighted to see her, she was sure of that. She also knew that Hugo had gained as much satisfaction as she had, working together as such a close team. Maggie had been watching for and hadn't spotted any signs of Hugo being upset in any way at Joan running off with someone else, but that didn't mean he was ready to contemplate a new relationship, did it? Especially not with her.

'Are you going home now?'

'No,' Hugo responded swiftly. 'I'll hang around till we get all the results back on Lucy's tests. We haven't managed to collect that urine sample yet and I won't leave unless I'm sure it's safe. Neonates can deteriorate rapidly, as I'm sure you know. I may end up staying here all night.'

'I could go and feed the dogs for you if you like. And maybe give them a run on the beach.' Maggie's glance at Hugo was almost forlorn. 'I'm missing them.'

'They miss you, too,' Hugo told her. 'They seem to have aged ten years in the last week. I think they're pining.'

'Oh, sure.' Maggie snorted softly. 'I was only a visitor for a few weeks. It's hardly likely to have changed their lives.'

'It changed mine.'

By an unspoken signal both Maggie and Hugo stopped walking. They stood in the empty and now dimly lit corridor and simply stared at each other. Maggie felt as though an unseen switch had been flicked, releasing a current of electricity that brought the very air they were breathing alive.

'I miss you, Maggie.' The expression in Hugo's dark eyes reached out to touch Maggie. To caress something deep inside her, in a place no one else had ever come close to touching. The whole world seemed to be holding its breath, as Maggie was, waiting for Hugo's next words. 'I…I think I might be in love with you.'

For a second, Maggie could say nothing. She could do nothing but hold the gaze and let the words sink in. Then she found she could breathe again. 'Don't you know, Hugh?'

'Well, yes. I do know,' Hugo admitted.

'And?' Maggie's eyes were locked on his. This was it. Time to take the risk. Here he was, knowing that he was free to love Maggie any way she wanted him to. And it was terrifying because the thought that she might not want him as much as he wanted her had the potential to destroy something Hugo knew he could never find again. But Hugo hesitated for just a fraction longer.

'Have you heard about Joan's engagement to Lewis Evans?'

'Mmm.' Maggie's gaze was still fixed on Hugo's face. 'How do you feel about that?'

'Fine,' Hugo said honestly. He smiled fleetingly. 'Relieved, really. Joan and I were never more than good friends. We both knew it wasn't the real thing. It was Joan, in fact, who tried to persuade me that you and I should be together.' Hugo took a deep breath. 'I've always loved you, Maggie, but now I'm in love with you as well and I can't imagine my life without you. I want you—more than I ever thought it was possible to want someone—but given our history I wasn't sure that I *should* feel the way I do. Or that you would want me to.'

'Oh…' A tiny smile plucked at the corners of Maggie's mouth and then grew. 'That's an easy problem to solve.'

'Is it?' Hugo was aware of an odd feeling. As though the air around them was crackling with something. A tension that was escalating with astonishing speed.

'Mmm.' Maggie's smile faded to leave her looking more serious than Hugo had ever seen her look out of a professional setting. 'I want you to feel that way, Hugh,' she said very softly. 'I want you to very much. I'm in love with you as well. I always have been.'

Hugo could reach out and touch her now. He wanted nothing more than to bury his fingers amongst those auburn spirals and tilt Maggie's head so that he could touch her lips with his own. And she wanted him to. He could feel it. That crackle in the air was desire and it couldn't be anything like that powerful if he was the only one contributing to it. Keeping his hands still was the hardest thing Hugo had done for a long, long time.

'I don't want it to spoil anything,' he said. 'I don't want to lose what we already have, Maggie. That feeling of family.' It was a small word but it encompassed so much. Emotional safety. Acceptance. A bond that could never be broken.

'We can't lose that,' Maggie said. 'It's part of who we are, Hugh. Becoming lovers would just give us so much more.'

Lovers. Even the sound of the word was thrilling but Hugo couldn't let himself think of how much more thrilling it would be to take the next step. Not just yet.

'I don't want to hold you back, Maggie. To tone you down. You'd hate that.'

'And I don't want to drive you crazy by being too outrageous.' Maggie smiled. 'Maybe we can learn to find some middle ground.'

'You mean, you dream up the wild ideas and I'll be boring and sensible and tell you when they won't work?'

'Mmm.' Maggie had that gleam in her eyes that Hugo loved so much. Pure mischief. 'Like, I could suggest that you kiss me. Right here. Right now.'

'And I could say that would be very unprofessional and we should wait until later.'

The eye contact wasn't broken even by a blink. And the movement from them both was simultaneous. And then Hugo's fingers were in Maggie's wonderful hair, brushing the exquisitely soft nape of her neck, and Maggie's hands were reaching up over his shoulders. Their lips met gently. Briefly. Once and then again. They drew apart just far enough to read the other's expression and then a kiss began like no kiss had ever existed before.

Not gentle.

And definitely not brief.

CHAPTER TEN

THE imprint of that kiss would be there for ever.

Wonderingly, Maggie touched her lips as she stood in front of the bathroom mirror the next morning. The memory of the kiss sent a thrill cascading through her entire body, strong enough to make her catch her breath in a faint gasp. Their first deliberately sexual contact had been all that Maggie had ever imagined it could be. And more.

And it had been simply a kiss. Some time soon, maybe even today, they could explore this new relationship further but Maggie was happy to revel in the excitement of the sexual tension without tarnishing it with any desperate timetable for consummation. That would come, as inevitably as it now felt for Maggie and Hugo to have come together as man and woman. The 'rightness' of it all was so powerful, it filled Maggie with a strange but wonderful sense of peace.

She loved Hugo. Always had. Always would. She loved his intelligence, his humour and even his inclination to be so sensible. He was rock solid. He had always been there to protect and guide her and to pick up any pieces when things went wrong. She had shared him in that capacity with Felicity but now he would be there just for her. The love that underpinned that protection would be very different, however. Stronger. And *so* much more exciting.

Felicity would have approved. Maggie could almost see her now with her dark brown eyes, so like Hugo's, gleaming with reflected mischief as they planned yet another stunt that would annoy and possibly amuse her older brother. Maggie was smiling as she finished combing her styling product through her damp curls. She would probably still annoy Hugo at frequent intervals but she knew she could still amuse him as well. She could also goad him into being more adventurous and finding more fun in life. He wouldn't be wearing a suit to the next fancy-dress party they went to, that was for sure.

Above all, Maggie could love Hugo the way he deserved to be loved. Maggie had no doubt whatsoever that they would be together for the rest of their lives. They would have children and dogs and live by the lake amongst the mountains in an area she had come to love as much as Hugo did. Maggie stroked a little mascara onto her eyelashes. How many children would Hugo want? Maybe they would need a bigger house than the shearers' quarters had become. And maybe they should live closer to Queenstown so that the children would be close to the stimulation of the town centre and its colourful, international flavour.

The knock on the bathroom door startled Maggie out of her daydream.

'You finished yet?' It was Sven. 'Lisa needs a shower before she goes to work.'

'I'm done.' Maggie left the relative privacy of the tiny bathroom and went to make herself a coffee.

'You slept in,' Jason observed. 'That's not like you, Maggie.'

'I was tired,' Maggie told him.

'Did we keep you awake last night after we got home?' Jason was grinning. 'Erin's new boyfriend, Micky, is a bit noisy, isn't he? You should have seen him at the club.'

'I didn't mind,' Maggie said. 'I wasn't asleep anyway.' It was true. Thanks to reliving that kiss and savouring the pure happiness of the permission it had bestowed to imagine a whole new future, Maggie had been wide awake until about four a.m. She had fallen asleep finally and deeply to find it was almost nine when she'd opened her eyes. Having taken her time showering and dressing, Maggie was now ready to start what promised to be the most exciting day of her life.

'We're all going out this afternoon,' Jason told her. 'Erin and Micky want to try the Shotover jet-boat ride. Do you want to come?'

'I'm going to visit Hugh,' Maggie tried to keep her tone casual. 'We'll probably take the dogs for a walk.'

'Mmm.' Jason raised an eyebrow. 'Exciting.'

Maggie grinned. A quiet walk with Hugo and the dogs sounded like a perfectly exciting way to spend a Saturday afternoon as far as she was concerned. They could go over the hills and along the beach and maybe sit for while throwing sticks for Seth and skimming flat stones on the lake surface. OK, so it wasn't particularly adventurous but it had an appeal that made Maggie realise she wouldn't want to live anywhere else even if she and Hugo had half a dozen children. The setting was like Hugo. Solid. Safe. It was home.

'Why don't you bring him along for the ride? I'll bet it's a while since he had an adrenaline rush like that. Doc Patterson needs a bit of excitement in his life, I reckon.'

'You could be right.' Maggie sipped her coffee and avoided meeting Jason's gaze. What was happening between her and Hugo was private for now. She didn't want her colleague to guess the kind of excitement she was planning for Dr Patterson in the very near future. She hid her smile. 'I'll see what he feels like doing.'

'Cool. We're going to go out for dinner afterwards and then back to the club where Lisa works. They've got a live band tonight.'

Maggie finished her coffee and rinsed out the mug. The idea of being in a crowd was totally unappealing. This was going to be their day. Hers and Hugo's. She didn't want the company of anyone else and hopefully nobody else would need Hugo's. When she drove past the hospital on her way around the lake thirty minutes later, Maggie was pleased to see that Hugo's Jeep was not in the car park. That was a good start. Hugo hadn't rung to suggest any changes to the arrangement they had made last night either so Maggie assumed that things at the hospital were under control.

Hugo confirmed that this was the case as soon as Maggie had finished returning the ecstatic greeting the dogs bestowed on her. 'Lucy's doing fine. It turned out to be a urinary tract infection but it was well covered by the medication we'd already started. By the time I left the hospital at two a.m. she was showing a good response to the antibiotics. Her temperature's well down this morning and she's feeding well. We'll keep her in for another day and repeat some blood tests, but I'm quite happy to leave her for a while.' Hugo was smiling. 'I'm free to do whatever you want.'

The wash of excitement caused by the expression in Hugo's dark eyes was followed, unexpectedly, by a peculiar sensation of anxiety. What was going to happen between them might be inevitable and absolutely right but it was still a huge step into unknown territory. For the first time in her life, Maggie felt acutely shy. She had to look away from Hugo and clear her throat to help her find her voice.

'I…I thought a walk with the dogs would be nice.'

'They've had a walk,' Hugo said. His voice sounded a little odd and Maggie wondered if her unease had been contagious. 'I thought you might like to do something a bit more exciting. Away from home. And then…' It was Hugo's turn to clear his throat now. 'Then we could come back here and cook some dinner. I've got a nice bottle of wine and…'

And they both knew what would happen after dinner. In front of a roaring fire, maybe, or in the longed-for haven of Hugo's bed. It hung between them. A tension that was delicious but nerve-racking. They couldn't just take that step now, in broad daylight, but it was hard to think of doing anything else. Maggie caught Hugo's gaze and knew that he was feeling just as keyed up as she was. Maybe more. Was he nervous that he wasn't going to be exciting enough company for her? Was that why he was suggesting an adventure of some kind?

It was a perfect solution. They needed some time with each other to get used to the idea of taking that step into complete intimacy. And the offer Hugo was making here was important as well. He was offering something adventurous. Possibly even bungy-jumping or jet-boating through the terrifying rapids the Shotover River presented. Something he might not be prepared to do for anyone else. And Maggie loved him for it.

'What would you like to do?' Maggie couldn't help teasing. 'Bungy-jumping?'

Hugo kept his expression under commendable control. 'If that's what you'd really like to do.'

Maggie grinned. 'No. I was just testing to see how far you'd go as far as excitement went. What about the Shotover jet?'

'Sounds fun.'

'Jason and Erin and some others from the flat are doing that this afternoon. We could join the party.'

'Do you want to?'

Maggie's expression stilled. 'No. I'd rather be just with you, Hugh.'

Hugo's face visibly relaxed. 'I'd like that, too. Let's make some sandwiches for a picnic lunch and go somewhere just by ourselves. A drive, maybe.'

'We could do the Skippers Canyon,' Maggie suggested. 'That would keep us busy till dinnertime and I've been hanging out for the snow to melt enough to do that.'

'OK,' Hugo agreed readily. 'Do you know what time the trips leave?'

'I thought you wanted us to be by ourselves. We can drive it.'

'But…' Hugo collected himself. Sure, it might be safer to take a dangerous road in vehicles chosen to cope with the conditions and drivers who did it every day, but suggesting such a course would be sensible and…boring. Plenty of people made the spectacular journey in their own vehicles even though rental companies specifically excluded the road on their insurance policies. 'But *you'd* better drive,' Hugo said instead. 'You've had a bit more experience than me.' He grinned. 'As long as there's no siren going, I'm sure you'll behave yourself.'

'Sure. We'll take your Jeep,' Maggie decided. 'It'll be as safe as houses.'

But the Jeep wasn't going anywhere. Hugo had neglected to shut the door properly when he'd arrived home in the early hours of the morning and the interior light had drained the battery.

'I haven't got jumper leads, damn it.'

'Neither have I.' Maggie watched Hugo climb out of the Jeep. It had been such a wonderful plan, too. Exciting enough to let Hugo know that she appreciated his effort to be adventurous and long enough to fill in all those hours until daylight faded.

'We'll have to take your car.'

Maggie blinked. Was Hugo prepared to take on one of the world's more dangerous roads in her little hatchback? With *her* driving? That demonstrated a level of trust that almost brought a lump to Maggie's throat. 'Would you *want* to do that?'

'Sure. Why not?'

Maggie beamed. 'I love you, Hugh. Let's do it, then.'

Hugo had taken his guide book of the area with him and Maggie had to smile at his determination to get as much as possible out of his adventurous afternoon.

'They finished making this road in 1888,' he informed her as they left the road that led to Coronet Peak well behind. 'We'll get to Pincher's Bluff soon and that was the hardest part to build.'

'Was it named that because it was a pinch to get through?'

'No. Pincher was the name of the road contractor.'

'We'll see if we can find a place to stop and have a look at it.' Maggie was concentrating on the single-laned, shingle road that wound into the canyon. The road was tortuous and the drop into the base of the canyon frighteningly steep. It was a little too close to the edge of the road for comfort at times and snow lay in drifts that obscured the edge in places, but there was plenty of room for Maggie's little car and the weather was gloriously fine, so there was no need to worry that the conditions would get worse.

'It took Pincher's gang two years to do a section just under three hundred metres long.' Was Hugo reading his book to avoid the view into the canyon's base? It was on his side of the car going in this direction. 'They had to lower gang members on ropes to chip away at the rock with chisels and hammers. Then they'd put some dynamite in the holes. They had to be really careful with the size of the explosions so they didn't blow up the part of the rock they needed for the road as well as what was on top.'

Maggie was quite happy to soak in the history as they wound their way to the end of the fifteen-kilometre road. They stopped to look at water-races and sluices left behind by the gold-miners.

'The Shotover River was dubbed the richest river in the world,' Hugo told her.

They stopped to stare in awe at the Skippers suspension bridge and the incongruity of finding such an engineering triumph at the back of beyond, and they took time to admire the restored Mount Aurum schoolhouse and homestead where they stopped for a leisurely picnic lunch. Finally they walked quietly around a tiny cemetery hand in hand and stopped to look at a gravestone with a few Chinese characters marking the final resting place of a gold-miner.

'I wish we had the Jeep,' Maggie said. 'We could have gone right up the Skippers Creek to Bullendale.'

'We'll do that another day. It would be a good walk but it takes about two hours and it would be dark by the time we got back.' Hugo raised an eyebrow. 'Even with your expert driving I don't fancy that road in the dark.'

'Fair enough. I don't fancy it in icy weather either and the temperature's starting to drop. Shall we head home?'

'Let's,' Hugo agreed. He was still holding Maggie's hand and he gave it a slow squeeze. 'Don't know about you but I'm starving.'

Maggie caught the communication both from Hugo's hand and the look in his eyes and she had to swallow hard. Hugo wasn't talking about food.

'Me, too,' she said softly. 'Let's go.'

Was it the thought of what awaited them when they reached home that made Maggie drive a little more quickly on the return trip? Maybe she was just distracted by Hugo's proximity and the fact that his hand was resting on her left knee. Or maybe it was the underpowered engine of her car that needed such a percentage of its acceleration capacity to get up a particularly steep section of the road that kept Maggie's foot pressing firmly on the pedal. It was just reaching its peak as they got to the top of the slope. The road dropped away again and they were suddenly going too fast for the automatic transmission of the engine to help with braking.

The left wheels of the small hatchback snagged the edge of a snowdrift and Maggie felt the control of the steering wrenched from her hands as she tried to brake and steer for the solid side of the road. The car slewed and spun and then Maggie knew there was no hope. The front wheels left the road and the belly of the car ground against gravel and rock as they headed for a dive towards the dizzying drop that led to the river snaking so far below.

It all happened too fast to feel terrified. Too fast for any kind of reaction. So Maggie had no idea how she'd managed to find and grip Hugo's hand so tightly. Her eyes were screwed shut just as tightly. At least they were going together. And it wasn't as bad as it could have been. Maggie would have expected a drop like this to be gut-wrenching, the awareness of gathering momentum overwhelming.

'Maggie. Open your eyes, darling.' Hugo's voice sounded oddly calm.

Maggie forced her eyes to obey but she could make no sense of what she was seeing. She turned her head and then felt the movement. A rocking that was anything but soothing.

'Don't move,' Hugo said softly. 'Not even a muscle.' He gripped her hand so hard Maggie felt her knuckles crack. 'We're caught on the edge. I think we're stable for the moment but we need to be very careful here.'

'Oh, God!' Maggie whispered. 'What have I done? I'm so sorry, Hugh.'

'Listen to me, Maggie.' Hugo's voice was comforting. They were still alive...for the moment. He didn't need to worry about Maggie moving. She was frozen now. Absolutely petrified.

'Are you listening, love?'

Maggie remembered not to nod her head. 'Y-yes.'

'We need to get some more weight towards the back of the car. I'm going to release my safety belt and then yours. Then we're going to tilt our seats back very slowly. Don't do anything sudden, OK? And especially don't try and open your door. That could change the weight distribution too much to the front.'

'OK.' Maggie closed her eyes again. She knew what would happen if the weight distribution changed even a little in the wrong direction. A prickle of perspiration broke out on the back of her neck as she felt the car rock again when Hugo let go of her hand and undid the catch of his safety belt. The release of her own restraint made her feel even more vulnerable and she couldn't stifle a whimper of fear.

'It's OK, Maggie. We're OK.' Hugo continued making soothing sounds as he slowly tilted his seat back. Then it was her turn. 'Reach carefully for your tilt control and lean back very slowly.' Hugo kept his hand on the back of her seat as Maggie somehow found the courage to comply.

Then they were both lying back, their faces only inches from each other. Tiny sounds of stone and earth being dislodged from the road's edge ceased and the car remained still. This felt safer but Maggie's eyes were still glued to Hugo's face, seeking reassurance.

'Now we're going to crawl into the back of the car,' Hugo told her gently.

'What? Can't we just wait here until some help comes? Like another car?'

'How many cars have we seen this afternoon, Maggie?'

None. That was how many. They had been alone on the road. It was a popular tourist route from later spring to autumn, but not many people were adventurous enough to try Skippers Canyon at this time of year.

'Even if we phone for help it would take a lot longer than we can afford to wait. We don't know how long the car can stay this stable. We've got to try and get out of this ourselves, Maggie. By ourselves.'

Maggie wanted to cry. She had done this. Hugo had been right to be cautious and now Maggie was in the deepest trouble she had ever found. And she had dragged Hugo along with her. And she was too scared to do anything.

'You can do this, sweetheart,' Hugo whispered. '*We* can do this together.'

He made Maggie go first. She felt the car move and heard the awful grinding of metal on rock as the vehicle shifted an inch or two during her crawl over the back seat and into the space beneath the hatch. Then the movement stopped again and all they could hear was the sound of their own breathing.

'I'm going to move now,' Hugo warned her. 'Then we'll break the window of the hatch and get out the back.'

The car rocked and slid a little again as Hugo eased his body through the narrow gap between the front seats. Maggie started shivering with fear and it was hard to catch her breath. She knew it would help when Hugo was close enough to touch again. His warmth and solidity would give

her strength, his words close to her ear would give her the
courage she could feel ebbing too rapidly. But there wasn't
room for Hugo to get over the back seat.

'You'll have to break the window, love,' he said quietly.
'Aim for the corner and move carefully.'

Maggie's mind went blank. 'I haven't got anything to
break it with.'

'Your first-aid kit's in the back there with you. Haven't
you got a metal torch or something?'

Maggie didn't want to move again even to reach out
and touch the kit.

'Come on, darling. You can do this.'

Maggie touched the familiar box and made a sound that
was a cross between a sob and a chuckle. 'I've got a win-
dow-breaker *in* here,' she said brokenly. 'How could I
have forgotten?'

The small stainless-steel implement was not much larger
than a ballpoint pen and it lived with the small torch and
artery forceps in the top tray of her kit. Maggie positioned
the blunt tip and then hit the end with her other hand,
compressing the powerful spring fitting inside. The sound
of the hole being punched through the glass echoed like a
gunshot and Maggie flinched violently. The view of the
sky and the top of the rock face on the other side of the
road vanished as the window disintegrated into thousands
of tiny glass blocks. The car rocked yet again and Hugo's
voice shook just a little when he spoke a split second later.

'Good girl, Maggie. We're almost there.'

And Maggie knew what to do now. She pushed at the
edges of the hole and the fragments of window fell away
in chunks until there was enough space to crawl through.
She moved as carefully as she could and Hugo moved at
the same time. He couldn't afford to have his weight anywhere near the front of the car as Maggie's weight was

removed. As Maggie's legs vanished through the window following her body in a fall to solid ground, Hugo dived after them, the need to avoid sudden movements reversed as the car teetered and then tilted forward and down. The movement of the vehicle caught Hugo's leg. He could feel himself being dragged up and he twisted sideways in a roll to pull his foot clear with only a fraction of a second to spare. He landed on top of Maggie as the back wheels rose over their heads and the vehicle vanished over the lip of the canyon.

They could hear it, bouncing against rock and tearing through scrub and gravel. Echoes of the sounds came back from the other side of the canyon like rolls of thunder. The sound was horrendous and Hugo gathered Maggie into his arms and shielded her head with his own until the terrible sounds ceased and they were alone in a silent world, holding onto each other as though they still needed to save their lives.

Maggie was crying now, racking sobs that released the awful fear of the last long minutes.

'Are you hurt, Maggie?'

She could only shake her head. It was going to be some time before she could speak. Hugo simply held her, his soothing words and stroking changing gradually until his fingers could brush the last of her tears from her face and his lips could stifle the last hiccuping sobs.

'We're safe, Maggie. You're not hurt and neither am I. We've got a bit of a walk ahead of us or a wait for help to arrive but we're quite, quite safe.'

'This was my fault,' Maggie said brokenly. 'I nearly killed us.'

'It was an accident. And we're still alive. I don't know about you but I feel rather glad to be alive. In fact, I don't think I've ever felt so glad to be alive in my whole life.'

Hugo's smile was only slightly shaky. 'I guess there *is* something to be said for being reckless.'

'No.' Maggie shook her head firmly. 'From now on I'm going to listen to you, Hugh. I'm going to be so sensible you won't even recognise me.'

'Oh, no, you don't.' Hugo kissed her gently. 'I love you just the way you are, Maggie Johnston. I'm relying on you to make sure I get the most out of my life.'

'I think I do need toning down,' Maggie said soberly. 'I'm dangerous.'

'Only occasionally.' Hugo smiled again. 'And when you are, I'll be there to get us out of trouble.'

'Promise?'

'I promise.' And Hugo kissed her again. 'You'll keep life exciting. I'll do my best to keep it safe. We're a perfect match.'

Maggie snuggled into Hugo's arms, oblivious to the discomfort of the shingle road they sat on and the rapidly deepening chill of the air around them.

'We're in trouble now, aren't we?'

'Not too much,' Hugo said comfortingly. 'I've still got my mobile phone. I'll call the police now and let them know there was no one in the car. I imagine that crash was heard for miles. They may be on their way here already and we'll be able to keep warm by starting to walk to meet them.'

Hugo helped Maggie to her feet. She found her legs were still wobbly and she looked at the scars on the side of the road where the car had gone over and shook her head in renewed horror.

'I nearly killed you,' she whispered. 'I nearly killed both of us.'

Hugo's grip on her hand was warm and strong. 'At least we would have gone together.' He turned Maggie away from the edge and kissed her again. Very slowly and with infinite tenderness. 'I don't ever want to live without you, my love. My first thought in that teetering car was that I'd missed out on the one thing I wanted most in my life.'

'Which was?'

'You.'

'You've got me, Hugh. For ever. You already had—you just didn't want it.'

'Well, I want it now. All of it. Just wait until I get you home. To our house.' His smile was a seduction all by itself. 'To our bed.'

Maggie finally drew in a breath that didn't shake. 'I can't wait.'

'Neither can I.'

'We'd better start walking, then, hadn't we?' Maggie looked at the long winding road ahead of them and bit her lip. 'I hope we're not too tired by the time we get home.'

Their eyes met and their gazes locked. They both knew they could never be that tired. They smiled and then laughed aloud as they joined hands and started walking along the road. They had cheated death. Together.

And now they were about to start really living.

Together.

LIVE THE EMOTION

Modern Romance™
...international affairs – seduction and passion guaranteed

Medical Romance™
...pulse-raising romance – heart-racing medical drama

Tender Romance™
...sparkling, emotional, feel-good romance

Sensual Romance™
...teasing, tempting, provocatively playful

Historical Romance™
...rich, vivid and passionate

Blaze Romance™
...scorching hot sexy reads

27 new titles every month.

Live the emotion

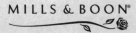

MILLS & BOON®

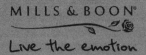

Live the emotion

Medical Romance™

LIKE DOCTOR, LIKE SON *by Josie Metcalfe*

He had a son — nearly grown, and so like him in looks and intention as to want to be a doctor too. GP Quinn Jamison knew that more than pregnancy must have kept Faith away from him for so many years — he couldn't believe she had fallen out of love with him any more than he had stopped loving her. Did he now have a chance to discover the truth?

THE A&E CONSULTANT'S SECRET *by Lilian Darcy*
Glenfallon

At eighteen years old Nell Cassidy was forced to give up her first love — Bren Forsythe. Now she's a successful A&E consultant, back in Glenfallon, and Bren is the new surgeon! Soon he rediscovers the fiery, passionate woman he remembers, and Nell wants nothing more than to open her heart to him. But first she has to tell him why she let him go…

THE DOCTOR'S SPECIAL CHARM *by Laura MacDonald*
Eleanor James Memorial

Dr Sandie Rawlings is faced with a challenge on the paediatrics ward — the gorgeous new registrar, Dr Omar Nahum. Omar has a reputation as a heartbreaker, and Sandie is certain she won't fall for his seductive charm. But when Omar makes it clear that she's something special to him, all her certainties disappear!

On sale 2nd July 2004

Available at most branches of WHSmith, Tesco, Martins, Borders, Eason, Sainsbury's and all good paperback bookshops.

0604/03a

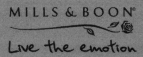